# THE BIRD FARM

*The Story of the AI and
Internet World We Live In*

Varun Aggarwal

Thank you for reading my book.
I have a surprise gift for you!

**'The Secrets of The Bird Farm'**

Access it by visiting the following link:

https://thebirdfarm.varaggarwal.com

*Dedicated to*

*All those who see imperfections in the world,*

*And those who have to put up with*

*such otherworldly people, their frustrations,
boring talks*

*and romanticism for action or, inaction*

*Like my family does.*

Chapter 1

# BC: BEFORE CRYST_ALS

*The bird farm is in no way similar to an Animal Farm.*
*Birds are a much more superior species than animals,*
*they fly.*

The sun was out, and the sky was bright with light. Birds filled the sky, as they do in the morning. They flew around, playing, making formations, and teasing with each other. Some flapped their wings wildly, some glided, some rolled onto their backs, just to do a quick flip and soar back high. And then there were the tiny ones with their moms and dads, learning to fly, while searching for a balance between their trust in their loved ones and the fear of falling. The chirping of the birds spun music. Their dancing silhouettes made the thousands of treetops, not one like another, rife with life.

Down there in the midst was one tree, a rather beautiful one, a rather unique one, where flowers and fruits of different colors and types all blossomed together. Birds of all kinds - who did not look the same, speak the same language or prayed to the same Gods - lived there together.

On one of the branches hung a small bird house, where lived a mother bird, a father bird and their daughter. It was a humble dwelling filled with a lot of books and large boxes of candies. On one of the walls, in a conspicuous place, hung a photo of a bird with a compassionate smile. This bird's name was Matma. Matma's story was made of legends of austerity and forbearance, as well as some strange ideas abhorring modern means of communication - for their ability to instantaneously deliver meaninglessness.

Bird Mustafa pushed his beak in the keyhole and flicked the door open.

"I am going to Sheru's place. Can you please lock the door, my Malika?" asked Mustafa.

Malika looked up from her book, "Yes, yes. And get the door lubricated, or otherwise, the day is not far when your beak will lay stuck in the door! Will spare me a lot of your useless talk, yet... And come home soon. My students will come for their teaching lesson in the afternoon. You can sit with Moshi then. She feels lonely in the afternoons. Her chirp goes away! She is still learning to fly. Falls every now and then."

"Oh my my, why do you always make me rush through these things. I have to talk to Sheru in quite some detail. He can help take my candies to faraway trees. Everyone loves them on all the seven trees next to us, but that does not make us enough money...  does it? Just imagine the day when the birds on all the trees get to taste Mustafa Candies. Their joy will know no bounds. And it can really help Moshi's future..." said Mustafa.

"My old man, you and your dreams. Sheru is not a good guy. I have not liked him, since I first met him. Why get in to all this trouble. We have enough for my books and you really have no expensive tastes! And Moshi will find her way. She is a nice kid – inquisitive and caring." She paused, and then said, "But, it is your business, so do what you please. I love my teaching and my students. And they shower so much more love back on me – it gives me a joy which nothing in the world could buy. My teaching record has been perfect. No one taught at Malika Classes has ever performed badly. Every year, I further improve my teaching methodology. My life is my students, their learning and my own. It is such a pleasure," said Malika getting slightly emotional.

"I know studying and teaching is your passion, Malika! But you can spare me all this emotional speech. I am flying off." Mustafa flew out of the house and paused on the limb he liked to call his balcony. He looked back, with dreamy eyes, at his small but sweet home, decorated with colorful flowers, figs and leaves. Then, turning forward, he spread his wings wide, fluttered them vigorously, and majestically launched himself into the air. He soared high, high, high and then dove down to one of the tallest trees in sight.

Sheru perched on a tall plant shoot, the highest throne. On both his sides, a minder fussed over a wing, gently stroking and massaging. All the birds in his *darbaar* perched lower down.    But, the height for each perch was very carefully and precisely decided: not an inch too high nor an inch too low. Once in a while the height of the perches would change - but after a lot of arguments, abuses, fights - both visible and invisible – a war fought for every inch. Yet, somehow the total height of all the perches remained exactly the same. Mustafa sat right there, curling his wings to make a seat for himself to sit upon. He felt nervous but never felt small.

"But, Mustafa Candies are loved by all birds. They melt in one's mouth like butter..."

"I hear that. Haven't I tasted it myself? But we are undemanding birds that like and appreciate simple things. The world is very different. Each tree has its own popular candy. Badshah candy, Bakri candy, Biteme candy and Whatnot candy. Who cares about us? Who cares about Mustafa candy or even who Mustafa is?" Sheru tapped his head with his wing twice.

"All the migratory birds, from the Oil Tree, Machine Tree, Colonial Tree, all of them have tasted my candies. They go crazy as Mustafa Candies melt in their mouths – crazy in the delicious sense, I mean." Mustafa continued excitedly, "and they all say they have never tasted anything like it anywhere. So many of them carry huge bundles of my candies, like babies, on their beaks when they travel over long distances. Believe me, it is quite tiring for them – but the taste has got them, and they willingly take all the trouble. And then my wife, Malika, do you remember? She did a study with the candies and has some sort of a report on their taste. I don't understand all of what it says. But, according to her, the analysis shows that birds love Mustafa Candies, much more than any candy around and they never get bored of it. We should at least try..."

" 'Try' is the word, my dear Mustafa. And if Malika says it is the tastiest, it must be. What a beautiful woman she is. We can try it just for her sake. But trials are expensive. I have to convince birds on faraway trees to try to sell it. They are always worried they will make losses. All my birds will have to carry the candies out to those faraway trees – it breaks their backs. And all the birds sitting tight here will have to spend hours working on this project. They have no love for me. They take big salaries. If I do not pay for a day, they will all disappear. And also, I have to keep Sopari pleased – the elections are coming. And after all the expenses and efforts of all my birds, what if no one buys your candy!"

Mustafa replied, "Aah! Sopari, I just saw her the other day. She was leading a flock of, I do not know, it was huge, a thousand birds. All flying in perfect coordination, following her every move, even before she made it. What a leader!" Mustafa thought a little and continued, "Sheru, I do not have money to invest. But I can... maybe... give you a very good deal. And you must consider, I am able to raise the price of the candies every year. That helps..." Mustafa's wings twitched as a shiver raced through. "How about fifty-fifty... to begin with?"

Sheru jumped off the perch, brought his wings together over his chest and began to pace up and down in small steps. "Mustafa, you are so naive. I run my business on tiny margins. Even tinier than this!" he said as he plucked a mite out of one of his wings, ground it in his teeth and flipped it high in the air. "I do no deals below thirty-seventy. You are my friend. Maybe I can offer you thirty-five." Sheru caught the mite in his beak and tossed it down his gullet.

As Mustafa was reflecting, a bird with a long beard flew down and put one of his wings on Mustafa's back. He whispered, "That is such good deal. I've never seen Sheru give it to anyone."

Sheru spread his wings apart and tapped his head twice, once again. "Yes, it is a great deal. But I don't like the name.

Mustafa Candies doesn't sound good enough. To sell these candies on the Machine Tree and Oil Tree, we need a majestic name... a real majestic name, which pulls like a magnet..."

"How about Sheru Mustafa candy..." said the bird with the long beard thoughtfully.

Just then, loud screams started coming from the outside startling all the birds.

Shadow after shadow of birds passed by and cast a shade over Sheru and the others in the palatial nest, as if drowning them all in a revolution. Sheru fluttered his wings anxiously a few times, and then calmed himself down for the moment.

The instinctive reaction of the birds was to open their wings and fly out. Still, the lower perches followed the higher perches in perfect order. Mustafa himself tumbled along behind.

Along a long tree branch, Bakru paced up and down. Sometimes he flew a little, sometimes he glided. And then he would start walking again, losing his balance every now and then. He had excitement written all over him. He carried tiny pieces of crystals with him. Every now and then he peered at them with amazement and hope. Sometimes he rubbed them as if a Genie would pop out. And sometimes in a mumble and sometimes in a scream, he would repeat "Now the birds will really fly... high. This is magic... fly high... not stopped by anyone! Free at last!"

All the birds from everywhere were flying in a rush to hear him. They flocked and settled themselves around him. Mustafa arrived and was surprised to see Malika and Moshi land as well. He looked at Malika questioningly. Her eyes answered back, "Everyone else was coming. Why shouldn't I?" To which Mustafa's eye roll responded, "And what happened to your teaching class – come early, nonsense?" He scoffed.

Hundreds of birds from all the seven trees were here. Sheru alighted in front of Bakru, who ran directly into his chest and became nearly apoplectic. Sheru stroked Bakru's wings and looked deeply into his eyes, signaling him to calm down. Bakru regained himself somewhat and began to speak.

"Magic has happened. You see these little glasses, these beautifully cut glasses... Actually not glasses... crystals... They are magic All the birds will now fly high, soar high, free, as nature had always designed, they cannot be stopped by anyone anymore. Real freedom is here. It will no more be like it is today – as if we all live in a bird farm!"

Bakru was out of breath and charged with emotions. He made a mighty effort to control his feelings, turned to the gathering throng, and began his speech. "My friend birds, I have news for you. Over all these years, these wings have carried many stories far and wide. But this is the mother of them all. And it is not some useless story of a royal having a baby, interesting gossip about an actor's boyfriend, a sensational sex scandal or some miracle performed by a God-bird. This is something, a real miracle, which will impact each one of our lives and change it."

He took a crystal in his beak and raised it high, moving it around so that every bird could have a look. Then he continued, "You see this crystal – it is magical. Such crystals have been spread across all the trees. They reflect images to each other. What does it mean? It means…"

Bakru looked around, spied Mustafa, and clasped him in his wing. "It means Mustafa can have a magic mirror in his house and share his reflection in the mirror with anyone he wants... the mirror will reflect his image to the other crystals in his tree, to the crystals in nearby trees, and to the crystals near to those trees, and so on until his reflection is seen even in the faraway trees. Everyone will be able to see his reflections... meaning everyone will be able to see him! Didn't I say it is magic?" Bakru's audience glanced around at each other and looked back at Bakru, puzzled. They thought he had lost it.

Bakru paused and then said emphatically, "OK, let me explain. Let us say Mustafa wants to share a message about his candies, or talk to his brother on the tree of Gods, he can just stand in front of the mirror, and start talking... his reflection will be carried on his command to whomsoever he wants! It is all a magic of reflections – these reflections will take Mustafa anywhere Mustafa wants to go. He can post his knowledge on the reflections, browse through information posted by other birds and communicate with any bird he wants, on the faraway trees." If anything, the birds looked more puzzled. But Bakru persisted.

"And I say to you that reflections are the new wings of birds! Reflections will take us far and wide! They are so much faster than our current wings, they fly at the speed of light! That is why we call it the World Wild Web. And think of it, Mustafa can now be present at one hundred places at once, without even leaving his home. If this is not magic, then what is?" Mustafa stood there blushing. He could indeed imagine that he was reflecting images: one of some importance and one of a fool. He twitched his wings.

Sheru shot back derisively: "Bakru, have you gone mad? This is so funny. Maybe you drank a little too much last night. Putting a mirror in Mustafa's house and sending his reflection to crystals? Now, how will Mustafa change his clothes after a bath. Do you want everyone to see him without clothes?" At this, Sheru had a hearty laugh and the birds followed. Mustafa managed a weak smile. Why did Bakru have to talk about him in the first place? And why did he elbow his way to the front to stand next to Bakru, when he could have just hid in the crowd?

Bakru steadied himself, smiled and replied, "Hahaha, NO, Sheru, I am not a drunkard like you. You are flying naked around all the trees all the time. Of course, you do not know nor can you remember because you are always drunk!

Everyone has seen you naked!" This got a meek laugh from the crowd. Bakru continued. "It doesn't work that way. Mustafa can control when and which reflections he wants to share. He can choose who he wants to share the reflections with – all birds, some birds or just a single bird. Birds will be the masters of their destinies. Now he can tell about Mustafa Candies to every bird on every tree, contact all buyers himself, sell everywhere. Oh, they are so yumm... Mustafa, do you have some with you? This is magic, let us all celebrate with Mustafa Candies."

As the birds were sharing candies and loud chirps were filling the air, a circle of birds descended from the sky. They pushed all the birds backwards and encircled Bakru. Sopari, the leader of the birds stood majestically. She snatched the crystal from Bakru.

"My birds inform me that you have been making speeches of some crystal revolution. By whose permission are you spreading this falsehood? Why didn't you appear in front of me first? Who owns these crystals? Who controls them? The owners need to talk to me before anyone can use them. Bakru, you have been made a fool and you are making fools of everyone."

Bakru was not the one to be intimidated. "Sopari, you can snatch a crystal from my hand, but not the crystal revolution from the birds. The crystal web needs no one's permission. Gone are the days when little helpless birds had to seek your permission. A revolution has happened! No one owns the crystals. They belong to the birds, they are everyone's. Each of these birds will incarnate a thousand wings, a million feathers, as they reflect through the crystal web. They will all fly high, wide, and free, what they were made for. No more in your clutches..."

Sopari pounced back. "But who regulates these crystals? What are the rules of using them? Why will it not be misused? They can be a big danger to all these birds that I love." She and her clan must govern them, like the way they controlled everything else.

"No, my friend Sopari, the crystals are self-governed – or as they say, community governed. This is what I was coming to... I hereby announce the commandments of the community!" Bakru jumped with excitement as he proclaimed each commandment.

*Do no evil*

*All birds will be treated equally*

*All birds will have a voice*

*No one will store or trap any reflection*

*All birds have equal right to buy and sell using crystals*

*All the birds will have jobs, none will be exploited*

*No one will own the crystals*

The branch shook with Bakru's every jump and then there was a crackling sound. Can a branch hold the weight of a revolution? The birds hushed and weaved but Bakru held his balance and smiled. "Old branches need to go, to give way to new ones, better ones..." Birds went into celebration, once again.

Moshi stepped forward to look at the crystal in Bakru's wing... so beautiful, so pure, shining splendidly. She had never seen anything like it.

Suddenly, a bird brought a crystal right in front of her eyes. "Hi, my name is Jaico! You can have this one." Jaico was a handsome young bird.

"Jaico, who? How do you have a crystal? Oh, it is beautiful, isn't it!" exclaimed Moshi.

"Eh! I have come from the tree of machines. Well, my father thinks I am good for nothing. He is a friend of Sheru. I have always been attracted by glasses and crystals. I have done a course in cutting them, polishing them and arranging them.  I have many of these. You can have one."

Moshi took the crystal and held it in her beak. She flapped her wings and took off...  to fly high, far and wide, without even a little slip, in the deep blue sky, as if in freedom.

# Chapter 2
# CE: CRYSTAL EVOLUTION

*Birds have wings, may this story have not. Let it move slowly, from one person to another, there is no hurry.*

**"Good travels at a snail's pace—it can, therefore, have little to do with the railways. Those who want to do good are not selfish, they are not in a hurry, they know that to impregnate people with good requires a long time. But evil has wings."**

- Mahatma Gandhi, in 'Hind Swaraj'

Mustafa and Moshi flew side-by-side, hopping from one tree to the next, sometimes circling a tree branch like a merry-go-around, sometimes diving through the narrow leaf lanes, and then competing to see who can soar faster and higher. It was so much fun for the father and daughter! The chirpy Moshi engaged Mustafa in a constant chatter throughout, asking all sorts of questions.

Mustafa, overflowing in love, was enjoying them all, even if he did not know the answers to all of them.

At top speed they glided into Sherman's shop in the big old banyan tree. Both were panting yet smiling. Mustafa had suffered a bruise over his left eye and some beads of blood rimmed his brow. Moshi was drenched in sweat, but she never really got tired.

"Oh, Mustafa!" exclaimed Sherman, slightly startled by their dramatic arrival. "And who have we got here, ah! Moshi has really grown!" Moshi responded with a shy smile. He flung towels to both.

"And what have you guys done to yourself? Mustafa, you are continuing your old ways... Just how you and Mori used to fly into my shop, playing your games and trying to outdo each other. And you had become too good for Mori, towards the end, didn't you...? So, let me ask like always, who won the race?"

Moshi looked inquisitively at Mustafa and raised her eyes a little. Mustafa just smiled.

"Oh! So, both of you won! Well, in the new world, I hear there are going to be many winners, isn't that right. And here is a candy for each of you. A crystal – shaped one for Moshi, and a star-shaped one for papa. And you know, don't you, that this is the tastiest candy ever," putting much emphasis on tastiest. "It is called Mustafa candy!"

Mustafa squirmed a little and said, "Sherman, my friend, you are so kind... always. It brings back all the old memories. Now, my girl here is looking for a companion, someone who can play with her, eat with her, sleep with her and always be by her side."

"Oh! So, she is looking for a friend, is she, well, we have so many nice ones here, and lucky coincidence, they are all looking for a good friend, too. And who would not want a friend like you, Moshi?"

Sherman guided Moshi to a large area with fifty different toys arranged in a neat 5X10 pattern. Moshi cautiously tiptoed into the first lane. On her left was a tortoise with brown eyes and a huge scary shell on his back. "Hmmm, perhaps too scary," Moshi thought. To her right stood a little squirrel with lots of brown fur and small brownish-black eyes. But this wouldn't do either. Moshi really liked nuts and the squirrel would probably eat them all, leaving none for her! She turned right, and her wing banged into a cat. He had big eyes, big whiskers and a big evil smile. A shiver ran up her spine, and with extreme caution she steadied the tottering kitty and quickly moved forward. Next was a two-legged upright fictional character, something out of sci-fi movies, with a victorious smile and carrying an axe studded all over with crystals. "Who would make a friend out of him?" she thought.

Feeling a twinge of disappointment, she moved forward. Around the corner sat a being who looked quite nice indeed. Here was a little bird with a small innocent face and tiny eyes. And weren't her feathers beautiful! She could see her own reflection in her glass eyes. Moshi glanced somewhat skeptically at the feet made of steel, but all in all, this friend was already a friend, and much more than a friend, she was like the tiny sister Moshi had always wanted. "I want this one," she chirped.

Sherman engrossed himself in tightening the screws on a toy duck. Spread out on his bench were a magnifying device, a battery, and a variety of spare parts. Hearing Moshi's call, he put down his tools and flitted over.

"Neat! You really have an eye, my girl. This little one was built by a scientist. He is a friend of mine. I often help in his lab. Do you know this bird can hear us and talk back? Here, let me show you." Sherman bent forward and spoke close to the bird's ear. "Little bird, how are you doing today?"

Out came a mechanical voice. "I am fine!"

Moshi stepped up and introduced herself. "Will you be my friend? Will you play with me? I have a lot of toys in my house."

"Yes. Yes. I don't understand. How can I help you?" came the bird's voice.

This sparked a hearty laugh, Sherman most of all. "She says a lot of crazy things. It is very entertaining! Never a dull moment! But my friend says she learns over time. Fantastical person he is - always engaged in his own world."

"Can I have her, dad? I really like her. I will make a little bed for her right beside me. And how will a little orange bow look on her crown?"

"Beautiful, Moshi! Absolutely!" said Mustafa, "Sherman, how much? And what is that slit on its crown?"

"I do not know the slit, but let me tell you a secret. My friend spent a lot of money building it. The money could probably buy my whole shop! And yet, he is giving it out very cheap, just a dollar. Crazy fellow! Just pay me in candies, no problem."

Moshi embraced the little bird with her wings. "Misho, my little sister! You are now my bestest friend in the whole world, and forever!"

"I don't understand," croaked Misho.

 "Oh! Mustafa, I see two of you! It is hard to put up with one..." Malika quipped.

Mustafa was standing in front of a magnificent and large oval-shaped mirror, hinged at the middle to a steel frame. It was large enough to frame both Mustafa and Malika and their big wings.  Little Moshi looked much smaller on it, sitting far away with a bowl of corn. And next to her sat Misho, mechanically dipping her mouth in and out of the bowl. The Matma portrait appeared there too, looking so diminished, almost like a speck of dirt. Mustafa even attempted to clean it off!

"Oh Malika! This is the magic mirror Bakru was talking about the other day. Isn't it magnificent? See, I look clearer in the mirror than I really am." Mustafa said pointing to his wings in the mirror. He playfully tilted the glass forward, backward, and then with a swift flip of his wing he sent the glass spinning end over end. "You see, it rotates on this steel hinge in the middle, like this. See these markings on the hinge and all these dials. Some have tree names, another bird names, you can slot in new bird names... this dial is for shops, and this one for information, and so on. You rotate the mirror and adjust the dials, and you go to different places. So here, let me move the dial to traders. And rotate the mirror."

Mustafa slowly moved the mirror upwards. Streams of reflections of trading birds began to appear in the glass, one after the other. It looked like a movie. Mustafa stopped at a reflection of a colorful bird with a beautiful tuft on his crown. "See, this is Poshu trader in the Oil Tree. He might be interested in selling my candies. Have heard a lot about him, but never been able to contact him. And here, I tap the mirror, sending my reflection to him... Oh my God! he tapped his mirror too... Wow! We are connected now." The reflection of a smiling Poshu appeared in the mirror.

Mustafa was caught somewhat unprepared, and he stammered with embarrassment. "Hello there, my friend. My name is Mustafa. I make Mustafa Candies. They are the most popular candies in all the seven trees around me. I wanted you to have a look at my candies and maybe discuss some business?"

Poshu replied politely, "Mustafa, I have heard about your candies. Many birds have told me about them... In fact, I tasted it when my niece carried it all the way to our tree. It is just the best!" Mustafa's heart leaped. "We have discussed about it and think it can help our business. We have been wanting to reach out to you for all these years, but how? And now we can. Good to see you today! I am in a rush right now. I just tapped back to make a connection. Send me business details and we will talk soon."

The colorful bird vanished from the glass. Malika stood there stunned. She was at a loss for words. Finally, she blurted, "This is a miracle."

"There are no miracles." Misho said mechanically.

Malika dismissed her with a flap of her wing. "Let me try to use it and see if I can find some good teaching lessons for my kids."

"Wait, Malika. Don't be so impatient. You will break it. Let me first explain. You tap to start your reflection and tap again to stop reflecting. Your reflection goes to different places based on where the mirror points and the dial settings. If you want to send reflections to everyone, just keep flipping the mirror till it takes 3-4 full circles. The reflection will go to all crystals across all the trees and anyone who is looking can see it. This is as much as I know. I am myself still learning. And now for your teaching lessons. Let us see..."

Mustafa began rotating some dials and adjusted the glass forward and backward a few times. "There, there, 'how to make a hanging nest,' is this useful?"

Malika looked at the reflection with amazement and then gave Mustafa a big hug. "Oh, wow! that is the most beautiful nest design I have ever seen. Mustafa, you are a genius. I will definitely add that to my class. Oh my, this mirror is really so powerful?"

 "Powerful things are dangerous." Misho croaked.

Mustafa cautioned, "One last, but very important thing. When you want the mirror to stop reflecting to the crystals, you just loosen the screw here at the hinge." Mustafa unrolled the screw to demonstrate. "There you go. The mirror is no more reflecting to the crystals. No one gets to see what we are doing."

A big conical glass flask stood in the center, atop a very large stove. The flask was full of crystals of different shapes and sizes, and of many varied colors. A number of beakers, and test tubes with liquids and chemicals were scattered everywhere. On the shelves sat crystals and small mirrors, all in disorder. Polishes of various colors and tools to cut crystals lay all around.

A mirror on a hinge stood on one side of the room. Opposite this mirror was another mirror that filled the entire wall. In fact, the wall itself was just one big mirror. It had reflections of crystals all over it. Some seemed to continue to infinity, suggesting the great possibilities latent in them.

Jaico held a chisel with his right foot. With his left foot he grasped a mallet and brought it down upon the chisel with gentle and precise blows. The chisel bit into a crystal that was gripped tightly in the jaws of a steel stand. Tuk-Tuk-Tuk, and a chip fell to the floor. Jaico paused and considered again the calculations he had made on a piece of paper. He put a scale on the crystal and marked a point on it with the blade of the chisel. Then he renewed the blows until another piece fell to the floor. He continued like this for an hour, whittling off piece after piece. Satisfied at last, he removed the crystal from the steel jaws and placed it on the table beside him, next to another crystal equally fine.

He then turned his attention to his polishes of many colors - red, blue, yellow, and green. He picked a crystal, fastened it in the steel jaws, dipped his feet in the red polish, and began painting its several faces with his toes. After covering almost half the faces in red polish, he let out a big yawn. He wanted to relax a bit. He flipped the magic mirror with his wing and brought up a sci-fi movie. The movie was about super-intelligent creatures, who walked on two feet, saw the world in all three dimensions, gave birth to full babies directly from their bellies, always wore something to cover themselves and had built something strange called a computer. They were cutting all the trees, leaving the birds with nowhere to live. He snacked a little while he watched. As the birds in the movie got angrier, he felt himself getting a little drowsy. Strangely, the super-intelligent creatures were puzzled why the birds were angry! Jaico's eyelids were shut.

Jaico bolted upright. He saw into his reflection in the mirror wall. The movie had ended around thirty minutes back. All of his polishes had dried up. He quickly washed them off in a strong shower of water and made new ones. Then he turned back to the crystal and rapidly polished the remaining faces. He finished in just a few minutes.

He positioned this freshly polished crystal between the magic mirror and the mirror wall. Any reflection in the mirror had to pass through the crystal in order to be projected on the mirror wall. While Jaico's figure was clearly visible in the smaller mirror, it appeared completely smudged on the wall. That is what the polished crystal did to his reflection – distort it. One could make out that it was some sort of a bird figure, but really nothing more than that. Jaico rotated the crystal slowly, and as he did so, the figure began to change rather dramatically. When he had rotated the crystal by a quarter, the image looked like a banana, a long thick line. As Jaico jiggled his wings playfully, bringing up one, then the other, the banana would tilt in one direction and then the other. He then spread his feet wide and held up both wings, and the shape transformed into an orange.

Amused, Jaico hurried to get the other crystal and positioned it between the mirror wall and the first crystal. Now the reflection from the mirror would have to go through both crystals before appearing on the mirror wall. The idea was that the second crystal will cancel the distortion of the first on tuning.

Jaico started rotating this new crystal gently. The banana bloated up in the center and became a bird's chest. Then legs began to take shape. Finally, the face began to form. The whole reflection flickered, as Jaico was trembled in excitement! The face finally appeared in full, but it was not sharp, and the features were not clearly distinguishable. As Jaico rotated the crystal further, the face began to disappear.

Jaico plucked out the crystal and flew to his math pages in exasperation. He flipped through page after page and began to measure the various faces of the crystal and examine their polish. Suddenly he stopped on a page and began reading it intently while scrutinizing the polish on three of the faces. He looked at the paper, then at the crystal, then back to the paper, then the crystal, several times. He then ran to his palette of polishes and re-painted two faces.

He hurried back to the mirror wall, re-installed the crystal and once again started to rotate it. First the chest and wings appeared, then the legs and then the face. The face had an evil grin. He adjusted the crystal a little more, or did he? And now the face appeared with full clarity, with Jaico's beak in its center, majestically raised.

"Eureka! I did it!" he screamed, fluttering his wings in excitement, smacking off the crystal he had just painted. He raced around the room from one corner to another, upsetting the crystals and mirrors and knocking over the lamps caught up in his jubilant dance. Finally, he collapsed in front of the magic mirror, completely exhausted. The chisel and mallet lay next to him and the polishes had spilled all over the floor. The palette had landed face down and mirrors and crystals crashed everywhere.  Was it creative destruction? Oblivious to it all, Jaico gazed skyward with eyes half-closed.

Suddenly, Moshi's face showed up in the mirror. "Am I dreaming?" he wondered. He stood up in haste and looked into the mirror with gentle wide eyes. He tapped the mirror.

Indeed, it was Moshi. "Hi, Jaico, did I disturb you?"

"No, no, not at all. How are you?"

"I am very well, Jaico, what about you?"

"Oh, Moshi. I am out of the world, beyond all these trees. I just built a crystal that changes the reflections when they travel through it, and then another crystal converts the reflections back to the original when they reach the recipient. I mean, when your picture goes through the crystals, it transforms, say to a banana, no one else could see you, and on my mirror, I see back my little Moshi."

"He-he! Me a banana. He-he! You built this for me?"

"Ha-ha! Yes, yes, I did. But this can be used for a lot of different things. One can send money through this crystal, without anyone being able to steal the money! No one gets to know any details of the money, the bird who sent the money or the one who received it. All of it is transformed into different images while passing through the crystal web. It is recovered back at the receiver's end, where a crystal decodes it. Isn't that great? Your dad can sell Mustafa Candies just through the crystals... no need of agents on other trees. I will build this into a business."

"That sounds nice. Though I do not understand it much. I also have some news. I got this nice little bird from Sherman's store. She is my little sister, Misho! I love her! She loves me. She talks sweet things to me. Let me tell you…"

"I only want to hear about you, Moshi. I am only interested in you, your eyes, your sweet little beak, your feathers…" Moshi blushed.

Sometime later, Moshi tiptoed slowly to her room after loosening the hinge of the mirror. She got into her straw bed and patted Misho, who was at her side.

"Sorry Misho, I came in late today. I was talking to Jaico. I love him! I am sharing this just with you. Do you think he loves me, and do you think he will love me forever?"

The mechanical voice replied, "I love you."

"He-he! You are funny, Misho."

"Do not laugh when I make a mistake. Teach me."

"Oh sure! You should have said, 'Jaico loves you. He will love you forever.'"

"Jaico loves you. He will love you forever," Misho reflected back, mechanically.

Malika stood in front of a mirror, not the magic mirror. She did not need the magic mirror anymore. She had a nice locket with a spherical block at the center hanging from her neck. Forty-two tiny diamond shaped mirrors neatly arranged side by side covered the locket in full. The mirror sphere hinged on a steel frame and could be rotated around with ease.

Malika had pasted nice black, white and golden beads in a very neat pattern on the steel frame. She adjusted the chain of the locket so that it lay just beneath her face. She took great care to bring the locket to a precise spot, tightening and loosening the chain, and making poses by turning her face to the right and the left, pointing her beak up and down.

Mustafa rushed into the room in excitement. He was about to call out to Malika, when he suddenly noticed the strange locket around her neck.

For a moment he was speechless. But he collected himself and joked, "What do you wear around your neck, Malika? Weird fashion it is, these days. And who is gifting you all this jewelry?"

Malika turned from the mirror, grabbed Mustafa by his wing and made him sit. The locket mirrors reflected numerous images of Mustafa's face: clearer than his reflection in Malika's eyes but lacking the same glow.

"Oh! Mustafa. Let me tell you. Just yesterday, I was teaching the egg lesson in my class. Shibu, Nasha, Itu and Misha were there. All of them are very good students and listen to my lessons very intently. I had just started teaching and was talking about how we keep our eggs warm in the winters. I made some sketches on how different birds sit on their eggs, based on the shape of the eggs and their preferences. This is one of my richest lessons. I prepared it by observing several birds across many trees, near and far. I have actually felt the texture and shape of their eggs myself and some young ones hatched, right here, directly into the cradle of my wings." Malika brought both her wings to her cheek in delight. "I have talked to the birds, discussed my observations, carefully classified the practices, reviewed, revised and documented them. Over years, several birds have studied my notes, used it in their lessons and provided comments, which I have meticulously incorporated to make the lessons comprehensive and accurate. It is the best lesson on the topic, I believe, across all the trees."

"Aha!" said Mustafa, somewhat bored by the talk, but also preoccupied with something else.

"I showed them thirteen major ways that birds sit on eggs, sketched each of them, and in fact demonstrated many of them." Malika bent a little, as if she were sitting on an egg, "It always draws a lot of chuckles! And then Nasha waved her wings thrice, signaling she had a question. She said, rather timidly, that she knows of three other ways. I explained to her that there can be thousands of ways, but what I have shown you are the ones most prevalent among birds. Small variations are possible. She sheepishly said that her three are the most famous ones in the tree of oil. And she stretched such a locket as this towards me, while it was still hanging around her neck. I looked at it in bewilderment. All the little birds surrounded us."

"And there, on one of the faces of the mirror sphere, reflections came right from the tree of oil. It showed these three very popular birds, one from sports, one a movie star, the third a singer, and the way they sit on their eggs to keep them warm. They were all very different from all my thirteen ways. I had never come across them in all my studies. Wow! I gasped."

"Mustafa, this locket is great! It is a miracle. It does the same things as your magic mirror, but it is so easy to operate. One can roll it, rub it and tap it with one's wings and the magic starts happening right there." She rotated the mirror sphere seamlessly with her wing, and different teaching lessons appeared on the tiny mirrors. "Your mirror was a total mess to operate. I can swipe around things effortlessly on this locket. They call it the *i-locket*, it amplifies the 'I', the Individual to the bird world.  And it is so small... You can just carry it wherever you go. Isn't it great?"

"Indeed it is magnificent. But handle it with care. We need to return it back to Nasha in one piece," Mustafa replied while coaxing Malika's wings off the locket.

Malika was a little taken aback. "Mustafa, this is not Nasha's. This is mine. I bought one today."

"Wow! What? I am sure this is mighty expensive!" Mustafa twitched his wings.

Malika lowered her voice a little. "Mustafa, I was too excited. Sorry, I did not discuss. I used my savings, all my savings, from my teaching of all these years to buy it." She comforted herself. "But, do not worry. I will improve my lessons quite a bit with the help of the locket. I am sure the kids will love my new enhanced lectures! I will recover all of the money, just in a year, by having a lot more students. You just wait and watch. And now do not get upset..."

"Oh, no, my Malika. It is all very well. You have bought no new jewelry since I remember. You are always engrossed in your books and teaching. And then Moshi takes so much of your time. You deserve to have a little something for yourself. And this locket is great. Beautiful jewelry and a useful gadget, in one! And I know you will use it for your studies, lessons and what do you call it, quantitative research. Once in a while, you must treat yourself to something fun, as well!" Malika blushed.

Mustafa continued, remembering what had made him excited in the first place, "And let me tell you, good times will come. There is so much interest in Mustafa Candies from across the trees. Do you remember that lad, Joke-u? I always thought he was a joker, a good for nothing, some crazy nerd. But he has come out as some crystal inventor! He has built this new system by which payments can be done through the reflections. Now, so many more folks are interested in doing business with me... business has already started on the trees of oil..."

The door flung open and Moshi dived in at full speed and glided right into Malika's bosom. Malika clasped her in her wings in affection. "I'm hungry, mom," said Moshi.

"Oh yes, yes, my daughter. I just forgot about dinner, in all these talks! Come, come, let us all go for it. And today, I have prepared a new recipe, coming from the tree of the sun. My locket gave it to me!" Malika exclaimed, while rubbing her new locket.

Moshi hopped to the table while Malika and Mustafa flew to the kitchen. Soon the table was brimming with food and drink. They dipped their beaks into their cups and raised them high up in the air.

"Good times are to come," said Mustafa.

"Good times are to come," cheered both Malika and Moshi together.

"Very good times will come," said Misho's mechanical voice, her beak rising the highest of all.

It was the darkest hour of the night. From high up in the sky, none of the treetops were visible. Everything silent. But from one of the crowns, there came a glow that is made of thousands of tiny points of light. The crown looked like a Christmas tree, woven through with glowing bulbs. Or like thousands of stars making their presence felt on the dark infinite sky. This glowing island, surrounded by thousands of dark trees, was the oil tree.

Moshi and Jaico flew side by side, flapping their wings in unison. They held a heart made of crystals in their beaks. Jaico had cut each crystal with care and Moshi had polished them in a beautiful kaleidoscope of color. Together they weaved the crystals onto a heart-shaped steel wire. The crystals reflected all the seven wonders of the tree world, in different shades. Jaico and Moshi looked passionately at each other with one eye, while enjoying their colorful background featuring the monuments of love. Jaico was a genius. He had fulfilled all of Moshi's dreams in this one moment.

And then, tiny lights began disturbing the reflections on the crystals. They looked like blots on the monuments. What was the source of these lights? Moshi and Jaico could see the tree of oil afar, its crown aglow with tiny lights. They looked at each other in surprise and then swooped down towards the tree.

Thousands of birds marched on the tree of oil, on every branch, the lower and the higher. There were lines of birds on all branches, marching in unison. More and more birds flew in and joined the lines of birds. Each bird held up a crystal in his or her beak, pointing it towards the sky, for freedom. The light from each crystal traveled to the many others, reflecting from them and back onto itself: reinforcing its light and making it sparkle. All birds saw the reflection of all other birds in their crystals, pumping them up with courage and passion. They signaled to each other through the crystals, directing which branch to go to, when to stop, when to march and when to hop to new branches. They were all coordinated, in high spirits and moving together to accomplish some goal. The lights reflecting from all the crystals lit up the whole tree and spread far and wide.

While Moshi held the heart tightly in her beak, Jaico quickly began to rotate and re-orient the crystals on the heart-shaped metal frame. On half of the heart he turned them to gather light from all the trees far and wide and focus it on the tree of oil. He turned the crystals of the other half to gather the reflections from the tree of oil and send them to the other trees. Jaico's heart was doing what hearts generally do – make connections.

Jaico completed the assembly and signalled to Moshi. They both took the heart tightly in their beaks and began flying round and round the tree of oil. They flapped their wings vigorously and flew faster and faster to gain speed. Half of the heart gathered light from the many surrounding trees and focused it to the tree of oil. This made sure that there was no dearth of light, the carrier of reflections, on the tree of oil. Light was necessary for the birds on the tree of oil to communicate with each other using crystals. The other half of the heart collected the reflections and the movements of the thousands of birds on the tree of oil and relayed them outward to the crystals on all the trees far and wide. All birds on all the trees had to be informed about the happenings on the tree of oil.

One reflection from Jaico's crystal reached Mustafa's house. Mustafa and Malika held each other tightly as they watched the revolution happening on the tree of oil on their magic mirror. Another reflection reached Sheru, who owned one of the largest mirrors. Sheru and Sopari looked at the mirror together, with eyes wide open and no expressions.

The birds on the tree of oil kept moving upwards, to higher and higher branches. Now they were occupying all the branches right up to the top of the tree, except for the highest. Meanwhile, another set of birds flew in circles, round and round, around the highest branch. They guarded the perimeter of the tree, leaving no place for anyone to escape out. On the highest branch perched a big red bird with a golden beak and large purple wings. This bird was surrounded by at least a hundred soldier birds, all with their beaks pointing downwards and wings aligned in an attack position. They had dipped their claws in the deadliest poison known to any tree: any bird unwitting enough to come close to them died in an instant.

Suddenly a light from outside flashed through the crystals of the birds encircling the top branch. Receiving the message, they all aimed their crystals towards the highest branch in unison, focused on the soldier birds and blinded them. With the soldiers in sudden disarray, another set of birds hiding themselves much above the tree, descended on the soldier birds. They drove their beaks into the crowns of the blinded soldier birds and knocked them off.

When the dust settled, all the soldier birds lay dead. The victors frantically searched for the red bird, but he was nowhere to be found.

Escaped, escaped, escaped, chanted the birds. Victory, victory, victory, screamed others, as they flapped their wings and danced around the tree. They cheered each other by knocking their crystals together.

Moshi and Jaico slowly deaccelerated. Jaico was exhausted. He reeled and lost the heart from his beak. Moshi was quick to respond. She held the heart tightly and balanced it, preventing it from falling off. Having known what had happened, Jaico quickly caught up with the heart again. They alighted on a branch, panting heavily, yet joyful. They embraced with a sense of victory.

As Mustafa witnessed the happenings, he caught a glimpse of Jaico and Moshi together, looking at each other. Sheru had seen them also: through a reflection passed on by one of the heart crystals, he saw the sight of Jaico rotating his crystals and adjusting them. And just then, the big red bird alighted next to Sheru and Sopari, stupefied.

"Crystals are overthrowing the dictators! Birds will be free. The revolution has happened," Bakru cheered silently to himself.

Chapter 3

# AD: AFTER DELUSION

*"Four legs good, two legs bad" – George Orwell*
*What about birds – two legs and two wings?*

A web of serpentine wooden tubes wound through the trees, intertwining with their branches. Each tube split into several offshoots, each of which further split until they reached into every house on every tree. Soulmates perched on these tubes during the festival of love. They splashed them with vibrant colors and engraved names and signs of love on them with their beaks. The tubes recorded these fond memories of love and togetherness. The deeper the engraving, the longer it lasted on the tubes - and deeper the love - the birds believed. The deepest of all engravings read "Moshi and Jaico - Forever." It was not carved by a beak, rather using a chisel and mallet. It was perfect, truly — neat, thorough, professional, without any room for imperfection, right down to the last detail.

The mesh of tubes carried water. No one knew for sure where they began, but they started from very high up. Some came from the waterfalls, some from the glaciers, and according to some birds, a few tubes descended right from the sky, bringing the divine waters! They had slits to deliver water to all the bird houses. The birds opened the slits using twigs hanging on them to get water for their daily chores. When they were finished, the water would just trickle through the floors and down to the ground, becoming one with nature.

Moshi stood below one such slit and opened it. A gush of water rushed over her and drowned her face. She jumped back. "The glaciers are indeed melting," she wondered.

She was wearing her mom's locket and tuned it to some music while she scrubbed her back. This music had been newly released on the tree of machines. Riding on the crystals, it came to her in an instant. She had recently begun to build a taste for such music, very different from what she heard on her own tree. It was so cool. She didn't even know, she had been deprived of it all this while. But now it was all so easy – the crystals were helping her discover her own tastes!

And how could music be reflected around? Simple – the music got converted into images, got reflected through crystals, and was then re-translated back to music.

She scrubbed her wings gently, then her legs, followed by her belly. She was pleased with her fine shape. She fluttered her wings few times to shed dead feathers and intruders. She then filled her mouth with water and swished it around. She was anxious to remove any shred of bad breath. Finally, she dried herself and tied a green scarf around her neck. After gently combing her feathers to get them in order, she stood in front of the mirror and looked at herself from every angle. She seemed pleased.

She smiled to herself and said, "My name is Moshami. I have studied all my subjects properly and with dedication. I am hardworking and willing to learn. I will do my best in this job."

"I will do my best at this job," corrected Misho.

"Thanks, Misho." Moshi pecked Misho on her crown. "Wish me luck."

"Very good times will come," said Misho.

Moshi soared high in the sky, all set to achieve her dreams. Her eyes focused on a single tree fully laden with fruits. She dove down to it.  The tree had a big crown, full of lush green leaves and so many kinds of fruit: exotic mangos, thorny pineapples, juicy oranges, lazy bananas and well, ordinary apples. One legend said that two mythical birds used to live in this tree. One bird bit into different fruits, one after the other. When he tasted a sweet fruit, he became happy, but when the fruit was bitter, he became sad. The other bird never tasted any fruit and never grew happy or sad, but just stayed content in himself. How did he quench his hunger? How could he be content with so many birds dying of hunger on the tree of poverty - Moshi thought?

A huge orange, fat with juice, hung on the tree. Moshi flew into the orange, but not in her usual style of diving at speed from on high and knocking the door open. She was prudent and watchful of her ways, as she walked into her new life. The orange was full of different birds, some pecking the orange vesicles, others collecting juice in small buckets they held in their beaks. Some were adding chemicals to the juice and stirring them with their feathers while another set pierced the buckets and collected the dripping concoction in bottles. Another bunch sat in front of tiny magic mirrors and talked to diverse birds from different trees reflected on their mirrors.

They talked continuously and without a break. They sifted through the birds on their mirrors fast, swiping out old ones and swiping in new ones, every few minutes. And then there were the birds, hundreds of them, carrying bottles of orange nectar, flying out through holes in the orange, to every place in the tree world.

Moshi was fascinated and overwhelmed. She flew around the vesicles, dodging them, while getting slightly inebriated from the fumes they gave off. Finally, she found her destination: a circle of five birds, all wearing glasses. She hopped into their midst and they talked, and she talked, and they talked, over and over again, for what seemed like a long time. They asked her questions and she did her best with each one. She answered some well, and slipped on some, but tried her best to be honest all the time. As her inquisitive self, she asked her share of questions trying to understand all she saw in action inside the grand orange, while weighing in her mind how much she would like to do any of these many activities. Yet, she kept an open mind to start with whatever she was offered. After the discussion, she was handed a bottle of fresh orange nectar and asked to wait. It tasted so much better than what she had at home. It was even sweeter than a fresh unplucked orange that she had once stabbed her beak into. Moshi felt satisfied with how the interview had went. All the preparation and excitement had taken a toll on her. She dozed off a little as she wondered about her new daily routine, and all the things about the interview she would tell Jaico.

A little more time passed, and then a bird appeared and said, "We are sorry. This job is taken. Thanks for the time you spent with us. We loved the conversation. We hope you enjoyed the orange nectar!"

Moshi couldn't believe what she was hearing. "But I think I would really like working here. I will put all my efforts. Please give me a chance to demonstrate..."

She was interrupted: "I am so sorry. The job is not there anymore. The management had a discussion and we have other plans."

Tears welled up Moshi's eyes. What did it mean that the job didn't exist anymore? She felt a heaviness in her heart. She had to share what had happened with someone immediately. Who would it be? It couldn't be her parents - she didn't want to disappoint them. She didn't want Jaico to pity her. Misho, yes, she needed to share it with Misho.

She prepared to leave. She turned back to have a last look at the place of her dreams.  And what - in the hazy picture - visible in her teary eyes, she saw a little bird that looked like Misho. Was she imagining things? She vigorously shook her head to clear her eyes and looked again, intently. Yes, she saw Misho, surrounded by the same circle of birds. It was no mistake. Misho had sat beside her all these years, and she would know her anywhere.

Discreetly, she tiptoed up to the circle of birds. Misho was at the center of everything, with her beak held high.

"Great, you have the job. You do it so well - no errors, so fast and with little cost," said one of the birds in the circle.

An older bird asked, "And one of the most important questions. Do you get tired? Or upset with customers?"

"I do not get tired or upset. I have no emotions," said Misho.

Moshi looked blankly at Misho.

All the birds in the circle broke into an applause: "Who needs the birds with emotions now! We have Misho."

And then, as if in final celebration, the small circular slit at the top of Misho's crown opened. From there emerged a crystal, hoisted on top of a steel frame. It shined splendidly, capturing reflections of the circle of the birds, the bulging orange vesicles, all the working birds, but no Moshi. She was not there – in reflections stored inside or outside.

Malika was on the fourth page of a book she had recently purchased. It described an experiment where some young birds were given lockets to see videos on how to build a nest, while some others were taught in the classroom. Each group had a random selection of birds, a few from every branch of the tree of machines. The birds were given a short test before the teaching lesson and another after it. The experiment's purpose was to identify which group learned more and by how much. It was complex academic stuff but appealed to Malika's nerdy leanings. "Who learned better?" Malika was excited to know and was reading rapidly.

As she turned the page, the locket around her neck vibrated. She tapped it gently and lo! the image of Jill popped out. She was wearing a scarf with long blue and red laces around her neck along with a festive mask. A trunk of a slender white tree, covered with red maple leaves, was visible in the background. Malika gazed at the laces in the scarf.

"Oh Jill, so nice to see you. You look so different and... where are you?" Malika asked.

"Malika, I am on the tree of machines. We all came here for a vacation. It is so much fun! A dance festival is going on here. Let me show you around." Jill lifted her locket in her beak and moved it from left to right. As she moved her beak , the whole scene came alive. Malika saw a troupe of birds chirping and dancing, another playing in a pool of water, and oh! there, who did she see but Jaico, sitting on his wings enjoying a drink with a straw in his beak. And who were all these other birds with him?

Jill flipped the locket back to her neck. "It is so much fun here. You, Mustafa and Moshi... all of you should come over with us next time. We will plan it together... Yes, yes, I am coming," Jill said to the side, "Trina is calling me to the pool. Let me talk to you later." With that, Jill waved and disappeared.

Malika was a little overwhelmed with what she just saw. Uhmmm, so where was she. Yes, right here, as she flipped through the book and turned her eyes back to the page. The locket vibrated again and without her knowing, her wings tapped the sphere. A song popped up. She hadn't heard it before, but she quite liked it. It was just right for her taste: soft, melodious and with an old-world feel. And then another projection popped up, this time a movie promo. A bird from a very humble background dwelling in the tree of the sun finds her way to become a movie star. This sounded super interesting, and while she was still looking at it, a third projection popped up. It showed a really wicked but enticing way to paint her nails.

Was she really rotating and tapping the locket all this while?

Of course, she was, she thought. The locket was such a miracle, it knew all her likings.

While all these projections saturated and competed for every bit of her attention, a final one came up, pushing all the others to the background. It was this tiny sweet bird, wearing red and blue laces, tapping her feet, dancing a little to the left, and then to the right, and back again... While she danced, the red and blue laces danced with her, to the left and then to the right, flowing like waves in an ocean. A constant smile lit her face. She asked, "Madame, would you like to buy this scarf made of silky red and blue laces, coming right from the land of the la la la. We have a huge discount on it."

"What a coincidence, I just saw a similar scarf and loved it," thought Malika. And they are also running a discount? She took no time to make up her mind. Malika's money travelled fast and securely through Jaico's encoding crystals. The tiny sweet bird promised to deliver the scarf the very next day, right into her nest. She wouldn't even have to take a step out to collect it!

Malika was so pleased with herself. Now, what had she been doing? She searched around. Ah! The book... she brought her eyes back to it and started reading the page from the beginning.

But as luck would have it, she was interrupted again. Moshi flew in, slowly flapping her wings, sailing very near to the floor. This was not her style. Usually she would soar to the highest point and glide in at full speed, throwing the door open and yelling at the top of her voice.

"What happened, Moshi? You look really low. You always come back happy and energized from Kiara's house. Now, now, you have been friends since childhood... what happened today?"

Moshi replied, "I am fine, mom. Just that Kiara went looking for a job and didn't get it. She had worked very hard for it. I feel sad for her. Anyway, I am very tired. I will go to my room..."

"But Moshi, did you eat anything..." Malika took several steps forward when her locket began to vibrate again. She brought up her wing to tap it... and Moshi was gone.

She went to her room and looked into the magic mirror. She had moved it to her room to prepare for the job. She turned it by an angle, focused it on the tree of machines and tapped it. Jaico appeared relaxing on his wings.

"Jaico, am I disturbing you?"

"No, no my love, where have you been? I have seen so little of you lately. I am just taking a short break. Powering all the crystals, managing all the reflections, too much work and a lot of responsibility. A lot of money rides on it..."

Moshi interrupted, unable to contain herself, "Jaico, I was preparing for this job, which I really wanted. The preparation kept me busy all this while. I had planned to tell you all about it, once I got it..."

She paused and then continued, "Today was my interview... I didn't get it..." She burst into tears.

"Oh no! Sorry to hear that Moshi. But why do you worry? Why do you need a job? You have me. We have no dearth of money. Reflections do all the work these days... and I control the reflections."

"It was not the reflections, it was Misho. Or wait... it was the reflections, or it was both, I do not know!" She felt confused and frustrated.

"Oh! yes, yes I understand all of that. We have plans for everyone. The community is going to give everyone money – no work, but money..."

"I like to work, Jaico, I want to learn – I like talking to people. I want to earn my money." Moshi replied, emphasizing the word "earn."

"Everything is reflections now, Moshi. Why do you worry, you have me. And I own the reflections. Do not be upset ... Let us leave these things aside. Come a little nearer to the mirror, I want to see you closely..."

Moshi stared at the mirror blankly for a few seconds and then said, "Another time," and dropped off.

She tiptoed back out of the room and fluttered her wings to catch Malika's attention. Malika was engrossed in the projections: the music, the movies and the makeup – She had never been so busy in her life!

Moshi looked around aimlessly. There was no one to share her grief. Strangely, her mind kept going back to Misho. It was her, to whom she told all her secrets, all her pains and all her dreams. She wanted her even though she was the reason of her grief or was she.

In her confused thoughts, her eyes fell on the portrait of Matma. It was still hanging in around, undusted and slightly disoriented. His smile, showing through the dusty glass, still appeared soothing and welcoming. There was a twinkle in his eye. Did he have a message for her? As if contagious, a twinkle brightened Moshi's eyes. She flew towards her mother's bookshelf. After a little bit of sifting through the books, her feathers getting stuck here and there, she got out a book with a picture of Matma on the cover. Her mother had been nagging her to read this book since time unknown. It had sounded boring then. Now was the time.

She waved with her wings to show the book to Malika in triumph. Malika sensed some movement. But then another tiny projection caught her attention, "Your Daily 23 Word Update." She tapped it.

"Young birds like to spend more time viewing educational videos than with teachers."

Malika exclaimed, "Oh! there you go, here is what I was looking for in the book." She asked, "Who learns more?" and tapped the mirror sphere again. "Young birds really love videos and are much more engaged." And then the 23 words were exhausted.

"Understood," said Malika, and she went back to the music.

Seven different birds attended to Sopari. Two worked on her claw nails, making them sharp, pointed and ready for attack. Another two groomed her wings, carefully cutting each feather, giving it a neat, but natural shape and combing out any intruders. Here and there, they plugged in a few red and yellow flowers. They hid a small twig among the feathers, without disturbing the perfect symmetry of her wings. Two birds stood on a small stool and worked on her eyes. One applied mascara around the eyes to make them look big. The other painted the eyeballs with a brush, giving them a green compassionate color. Yes, that is what Sopari wanted – big compassionate eyes. Yet another bird worked on her crown, painting subtle concentric circles with a fluorescent glowing paint. It gave a much-deserved halo to Sopari's majestic personality.

All of this started at five in the morning. Sopari always rose up early and worked really hard. Finally, at noon, Sopari was ready to go. She flew to her gigantic mirror. This was a mirror of mirrors, having an incredible shine, reflecting light in all the directions. It was effulgent like a thousand Suns, much like a manifestation of God! It was made of tiny mirror arrangements - each arrangement had some mirrors pointed downwards, some towards the right, some to the left, some straight to the front and some upwards. The arrangements were replicated again and again, organized in a nice symmetry, to construct the whole mirror. Together, it had a thousand odd tiny mirrors.

Sopari dashed in front of the mirror and filled all the tiny mirrors with her reflection. She was everywhere. She struck a pose to see the feathers on her left. She then posed right. She brought each of her claws close to the mirror, opened it in full and examined all the nails carefully. Finally, she blinked her eyes a few times and opened them wide, as much as she could, and admired how they looked in the mirror. Wow! she did look like her real self.

She turned towards her close confidant, Tima and signaled to start. All the seven birds were pushed out in a hurry, their fruits falling off their beaks, tumbling over each other – and they were gone within seconds. She couldn't tolerate even an iota of their reflection adulterating her's in the mirror.

Tima flew in and perched right on top of the mirror. From this vantage, Sopari could see Tima clearly, but she wasn't visible in the mirror at all. Tima flapped his right wing four times and the left one twice.

Sopari tilted the mirror a little and tapped it gently. In a split of a second, a thousand different birds appeared on the mirror. They were birds of all kinds – of different colors, of different sizes, with different beaks, eyes, wings and some didn't even look like birds!

Sopari  majestically opened her wings in full. She appeared larger than life. She brought her wings back in gently, jerked each claw once, and raised her beak high up towards the sky.

The birds on all the tiny mirrors were mesmerized:

*The birds that appeared on the mirrors pointed downwards came from the trees of crime. They saw Sopari's firm and sharp claws as ready to dash out terrorists from their trees.*

*The birds on the mirrors pointed to the left and right came from the trees of pollution (yes, they existed). They saw Sopari's nature-loving flowery wings as proof of her dedication to improving the environment.*

*The birds on the mirrors pointed straight came from the tree of poverty. They only saw Sopari's large compassionate eyes, and her eagerness to help the poor and downtrodden.*

*The birds on the mirrors tilted upwards came from the tree of Gods. They alone recognized the avatar in Sopari.*

But no bird saw Sopari in her entirety - it was just too much to behold her in full.

She began to speak: "My dear birds, my many thanks to all of you for being here. I know you all wish to talk to me... err... hear from me. I keep very busy as I am always working for the welfare of the birds. On the request of all of you, I have hurriedly come and stood here in front of you, uncouth and unprepared. Please pardon my appearance. Actually, appearances do not matter. So said the great Matma." She fluttered her wings and a small dirty twig fell off.

"We have to all work very hard for the birds and improve their lives. I want all of you to start using your mirrors and lockets very actively - spend more time on them than anything else - do not give it a miss, even for a day, do it like you do your prayers. I will be sending you reflections of all the work I am doing - I am always working for the birds - reflections know it all. The reflections of me feeding the poor, hugging the leaders of different trees, of directing the soldier birds to uproot the enemies, visiting the Gods and many more. You have to carry them to all the birds. When we reflect - we get solutions! So, all of you need to reflect … And the more you reflect, the closer you will come to me, the closer you will come to power. As I said, we all need to work very hard for the birds." And Sopari went on and on for a total twenty-nine minutes.

And when just a minute was left, Tima flapped his wings again, rather rapidly, making a funny noise to catch the attention of a Sopari so completely engrossed in her speaking.

Sopari ducked in alarm. Was a terrorist attacking her? She stole a glance at Tima. Then she gently got up, as if rising from a prayer and touched her crown with her wings.

"Thank you, God. We may all have your blessings. Thanks all my birds. Let your reflections take flight. Remember, my reflections take flight through you. Does anyone have a question?" And three mirrors from the tree of poverty, two from the tree of pollution, one from the tree of terrorism and none from the tree of God, lighted up.

Sopari looked deeply into the mirror with her big compassionate eyes opened wide. "Ah! no questions. And we are running out of time, Thank you my dear birds!" She tapped the glass and the mirror dimmed.

Tima sighed in relief and flew down to land next to Sopari. "That was great! You were better than all the twenty-eight rehearsals we did, seven for every kind of mirror. You fire up in front of the real mirror!"

"I just work hard," Sopari answered. "Now let us talk to the crystal guy. He said he can help us do a lot more..." Tima moved around the dials of the mirror, tilted it towards the horizon and tapped it. Soon a voice came across to greet them. Sopari and Tima got down to business.

Tima began dismissively. "So tell us how can you help us. We have been doing this stuff for years, even before you were born! We know the needs and greed of birds on each and every tree. Sopari has a great connection with all the birds. She delivers the messages they want to hear, and she does it with splendor. Earlier today, she delivered such a message going to every tree. She rides on the reflections now. What more is there to do? We have it all covered."

"Reflections are amazing. They actually reflect much more than you can see," said the voice on the other side. "You can tell a different story to every bird, rather than a story for every tree. Every bird deserves to be treated differently."

"And my dear little birdie, how will you know what every bird needs to hear? You reside in their heart or something, are you God?" said Tima scornfully.

"Reflections read their hearts, and they know what the birds even do not know about themselves! I know, for example, that the bird on the twelfth tiny mirror today, the one from the tree of pollution, is actually very religious... you gave her the wrong message."

"And how do you know that, Mr. Astrologer?" demanded Tima.

"Simple! Because, for eighty-six days in the last three months, every morning, her reflection went to the tree of Gods."

"Wait!" said Sopari, "How do you have her reflections? Bakru had said that no one will store or trap any reflection..."

"No, it was not that. You remember it wrong. The community trusts the reflections. They say, 'No one will let their reflection be stored or trapped.' But the birds do not comply! They give their consent."

Sopari said thoughtfully, "Hmmm... That sounds right! These birds can be an undeserving lot. But we need to work for their welfare. We need to educate them. I do so much for the birds – each of them needs to hear precisely how I address their concerns. What you are suggesting can be so very helpful. What do you think Tima?"

Before Tima could say anything, the voice continued, "And I know that 28% of your birds today got the wrong message. I have juiced the reflections for you. I know that the birds who wake up early, who play fewer sports, who wash their claws every day, are more religious than others. The reflections of these birds do not go to the tree of Gods, yet I know! You need me!"

"What rubbish, what is all this, black magic? I do not trust a word. Sopari, we need to be careful of this little birdie here! You have a reputation!" blasted Tima.

"It is called regression, my big Ostrich... Other than all of this, I also know you are attracted to birds with a well-formed belly, slender pointed wings, blue colored beak, small claws that can tickle your..."

"Stop there! Right there! I believe you," said Tima and flew off in a sulk, embarrassed.

The day was coming to an end. All was at peace. Sopari retired to her room. She threw open her artificial claws and crashed backward on the bed, with her little claws pointing to the stars.

Mustafa stood in front of the magic mirror. He had begun to feel small in front of it. A big GoodWeb candy popped out of the mirror. It was larger than life yet looked real. The candy was dripping with juices, and it rotated all around showing itself from every angle, ready to tickle one's taste buds.

Mustafa swiped the mirror to the right, and a little bird popped out of the mirror holding a Goodweb candy. The bird looked so much like Moshi that Mustafa felt confused. The bird also looked sad and depressed, "somewhat like Moshi lately," thought Mustafa. She slowly opened the wrapper off the Goodweb candy, slipped it through her beak, and quickly became quite animated. Her eyes popped out in sheer delight and she began to dance with happiness. The scent of the candy travelled from her mouth to another bird, her boyfriend, who had just rejected her. He flew with dreamy eyes following the scent and his beak met that of the dancing bird. They kissed and danced together happily, and the little bird tilted her head to the side and said, "Goodweb candy is the tastiest I have ever had. It attracts. I love it!" and winked.

Mustafa swiped the screen to the left and wow! here was the famous dancing bird from the tree of oil, the legendary acting bird from the tree of machines and the award-winning sporty bird from the tree of the sun. The Goodweb candy was at the center of them all, everything. They danced in a circle around it, dodged in and out, trying to snatch the candy and keep others away. But, lo! it was revealed that there was not one candy but three, hiding in a pile, ready to quench the desire of all the three birds. There were enough Goodweb candies for each and every bird that existed – both for their needs and their greed - no bird on any tree should be left wanting. The three birds celebrated their camaraderie cultivated by their love for Goodweb candy and expressed divine bliss on having their share.

Then Mustafa swiped the mirror in the upward direction and a bird wearing a tie appeared. He said, "Mr. Mustafa, I understand you are in the candy business. Would you like to sell Goodweb candies on your tree?" Mustafa's temper soared. He banged the mirror with both his claws and shook it vigorously. It was a rare sight of aggression from an even-tempered Mustafa. A thousand reflections of the Goodweb candy danced on the mirror, making them appear even more enticing.

He took a deep breath, paced twice around the room and returned back to the mirror. He began making some adjustments. He set some knobs precisely and moved the mirror around. With gentle movements, he tuned it to the desired direction. There appeared now a picture of a few little birds sitting on a branch with colorful flowers of his own tree. They were eating Mustafa Candy and smiling. What a heart-warming scene! A smile came back to Mustafa's face. Yet again, down at the bottom-right, he found a dangling Goodweb candy with a price tag.

He felt defeated. He sighed and twitched his wings. Malika came in rubbing her locket, looking rather pleased. "What is going on, Mustafa?" she asked.

"Not much. What about you?" Mustafa answered rather blankly.

"You know, in my class today, I was not getting any response from the students. Such a bright lot and no interest?! So, I looked closely, and one was rubbing his locket, another tapping it, and see the audacity of this one, whispering to a reflection coming out of the locket! I immediately took away all their lockets. In the process, I sneaked into one and saw this nice reflection of two birds romancing and talking to each other sweetly, on a private beach of a multi-starred resort, with drinks on their side, enjoying the sunset... I'm almost embarrassed to say I've watched it thirteen times since pulling it away from the student! Could not concentrate on the class anymore... Oh, well. Do you remember how many years it has been since we got married? No, you do not remember anything and when did we last have a vacation? You need to give me some more attention ... "

"Can you talk sense at least some of the time? Lockets, beaches, vacations, drinks... that is all you think about?" Mustafa bleated out.

In a feign of shock, she answered, "Do you have any manners? Is this how you talk to your wife...?"

"What manners? Romance, manners, etiquettes, these are the luxuries of good times. Is this all you worry about? Someone can be having a problem...!" Now Mustafa was almost shouting.

They both paused, squinted at each other and withdrew to their usual corners, stomping their feet a bit as they moved. They lingered there for some time, nursing their own sense of offense while carefully regarding the other. Their mind wandered to the recent happenings. How did they reach such a point? Finally, Mustafa stood up, which was Malika's cue to walk over to him and ask gently, "What is the problem you are talking about?"

"Well, it is bad news." Mustafa felt small. He continued, "No one is interested in Mustafa candy anymore. It is the Goodweb candy everywhere... Reflections are full of Goodweb candy. They do not like to carry Mustafa candy at all. I wonder why?"

He went on. "Lying in the corner, I was recalling what Bakru had said. In his seven commandments of the community, one was 'Everyone will have an equal right to buy and sell using the crystals.'"

"Oh did he? Let me see what the reflections say about it," and Malika rotated the mirror sphere. "No Mustafa, you remember it wrong, it reads 'Everyone will have a right to buy and sell equal to the money they spend on the crystals.' All the reflections carry this commandment. And it says there were only four commandments. You have surely got it all wrong, old man."

"Uhm! You are right, I am getting old," said Mustafa glancing at his white feathers. "Yes, indeed. They were four. I was confusing it with the seven vows of our marriage..."

"But tell me do the Goodweb candies taste good? Does it taste much better than our candies?" asked Malika.

"The reflections say its taste is the best, the best in all-times, all times that have gone, all times that are to come; all reflections carry it. I have never tasted it."

Malika put her wing on his and shook him. "But is that the truth? Remember, the recipe for our candy comes from your father. Who doesn't vouch for your father's creative genius among the seven trees around ours? And remember the study

I helped you with. You spent hours in the kitchen creating different variations of the recipe. We gave them to different little birds, and they told us how much they liked each one of them. Then you made more variations of the ones they liked and added some ingredients that none other know about. I continued the experiment with more birds, till we came to a very good taste. And do you recall, I did not stop there. I gave the best tasting candies to birds across seven trees and studied how they felt about it for the next three months. I still have the report around here somewhere. I am sure no one has done so much research with their candies. That is why I ask if it is true that Goodweb candies are the best, or is it just that they are everywhere?"

"I do not know or understand these studies. All the reflections are of Goodweb candies only." And then added, "Don't you know, reflections are the TRUTH."

Before Malika could say anything more, an image of Jaico sprung up from the magic mirror. Oops! Mustafa had forgotten to loosen the hinge of the mirror. A chill went through his spine... What all reflections had gone out? But, he was a little comforted on seeing Jaico.

"Moshi, come, Jaico is on the news..." shouted Mustafa.

Moshi came out with a book tucked under her wing. They all gazed at the mirror.

"Jaico, we welcome the star of the crystal revolution. Your colored crystals have changed the way business happens. Today, all the trees are doing business with each other. What are you planning to do next?"

Jaico beamed and spoke jubilantly. "Crystals are everything. And now we have the learning toy birds. The next revolution is when these two come together. It will solve all the problems. Everything will become very efficient. That is the future."

"This sounds very intriguing. But, what about all the naysayers. They say people are losing their businesses and young birds are not getting jobs. They say that all this is happening because of the crystals and the toy birds. Do you agree? Wasn't the promise 'All birds will have jobs, none will be exploited'?"

"No, no, these are stories being planted by those with vested interests. I don't know of even a single bird who lost a job." And he added an off-hand remark, "Please check the reflections. They say, 'All *capable* birds will have jobs, they won't be exploited.'"

Moshi stared blankly at the reflection. At this point, Malika's locket buzzed again. It was her daily update: "Goodweb candies taste the best across all the trees."

"Oh? And who says so? Is there a study?" she asked.

"Several studies, celebrities from twelve different trees and several thousand little birds. And your word limit is over," said the reflection.

"Ah! Understood." Malika finally got her answer.

The crystal heart was flying once again, around Moshi's and Jaico's necks. The sky was lit with stars. A nice romantic song, a new arrival on the tree of machines, was buzzing. It touched Jaico's heart the first time he heard it. Scenes from stories of love popped from the various crystals.

Jaico rubbed his beak on Moshi's neck, "Moshi, I will never forget the first time we met. I was recalling today how Bakru got us together – nice fellow, loves to talk about the crystals. All these days, we have spent so much great time together. I think about you all the time. Thanks for being there." He paused, holding his breath, wondering with nervous anticipation how Moshi would answer.

"I saw you on the news the other day." Moshi stared in the blank.

"Oh yes! Did you? Got to do these things. They never leave us alone. I do not enjoy it at all and I think I am not very good at them … But people say they like how I speak." He said in an off-hand manner, and then continued, "But I like you…"

"I heard you say that crystals are everything. They will do everything… change the world…" And Moshi gently nudged their direction to the tree of oil.

Jaico replied, "Oh yes! Certainly, crystals are everything today. Reflections are so powerful. Birds love them. They take their messages, they connect them, they deliver anything they want in a jiffy, all the information is available at a mere tap. Reflections carry information, the truth, to all places. It is causing revolutions. Don't you remember - we have been there - right here!" Jaico pointed to the tree of oil.

He continued excitedly, "And Moshi, this is just the start… I am working on a stealth project to get the learning bird to understand the reflections, communicate on the reflections, and operate, I mean, control the reflections…"

As the tree of oil came into view, Moshi gazed over its burnt leaves and broken branches. They glided through a swarm of directionless birds: many hanging upside down, some wailing, some dying, others tapping their crystals long into the night. Utter chaos!

"But, how is all of this any good? I see the crystals taking away jobs. I see crystals hurting my father's business..."

"There are jobs aplenty for those who are *capable*. My friends are doing extremely well. Earlier no one valued them. The businesses of the capable are flourishing..." He felt a little irritated to be challenged again and again. He had imagined having a very different conversation today.

"Who are the capable?" Moshi wanted to know.

"Those who understand crystals, those who can work with the reflections, those who can teach a learning bird; birds need to work hard to learn these things, they need to be smart, they need to invest in understanding all these new things... In the new world, everything is for the hardworking birds, the ones who are ready to take initiative, the ones who are ready to struggle, the ones who are ready to spend hours with crystals without a break. I must add, the birds who are not doing well are the lazy ones..."

They now approached the tree of poverty, a neighbor to the tree of exploitation.

"But why all this attention to the crystals? Will they solve all our problems? What about the birds from the tree of poverty? And the trees of hunger, exploitation, illiteracy, and have you thought about the tree of crime? And what if there is a pandemic? Will reflections address all of these?"

"Reflections will solve all these problems and many more. Reflections are the solution to everything. For all these years, problems were waiting to be solved by the crystals. The time has come. We just need to give all these birds a locket. They will be emancipated! Lockets are the *nirvana* for the bird world!" Jaico liked it when he got himself excited.

"And what about those who are just not interested in crystals?" Tears were welling up Moshi's eyes.

The couple was now approaching Moshi's home tree and it grew larger and larger in their sight. The tube with the deepest engraving of love had developed cracks. The imperfect tube, used to the soft pecking of beaks, couldn't bear the sharp and precise blows of the mallet and chisel. Tears had begun to bead up on it through the leaks.

"There is no future for them!" Jaico said rather spontaneously.

Regretting what he had just said, he turned to Moshi: "Oh! We have plans of giving all of them some money. They will be fine. And why are you worrying about all of this. You have me – and I am the master of crystals and reflections. I am planning to start my charity and I want you to run it! A charity which will use crystals to solve all the problems you mentioned. It will also help you learn something about the crystals! What more could you want? Are you in?" He raised a wing, as if to pluck something from the crystal heart.

Moshi looked at Jaico, as if for one last time and shed a tear. And then she let go of the heart from her neck and flew off. For a second, the heart dangled on Jaico's neck, but he couldn't hold it on his own. Down it fell through the trees, smacking each branch as it went. It collided with the ground out of anyone's view, and he heard it shatter into a thousand pieces.

Crystals, crystals everywhere, broken crystals of a broken heart, soft romantic music still piping through.

To one side lay a crystal ring, unknown and alone.

There was a long queue of birds, bird after bird, lining all the branches of the tree. Some even balanced themselves on the trunk of the tree, zigzagging down to a long line on the ground, waiting for their turn. They bubbled with excitement. It was worth the wait, yet their eagerness overtook their patience every now and then. At times, they would all break into a song and celebrate. At other times, they would just wait and count the minutes. There was no revolution happening here – just the evolution of the birds.

At the top of the tree was a big castle. The queue ended here. A bird came out of the castle, walking dandily, and feeling important about himself. His poses were welcomed by a sea of blinding flashes. A reporter bird came up with a mic and asked, "Sboj, long queue to buy the new locket. Birds line up here even before they wake up in the morning, just to get their hands on the device you invented. How do you feel?"

Sboj put on a smile, took the mic and angled it exactly. "I am glad we have given the birds an opportunity to walk. Poor things, flying all the time! We really worry about our customers and wish to give them the best with every new locket. The new locket will let the birds stand STILL... from flying to walking to standing still... they do not need to go to watch sports, go out on a date, window shopping, look out for theatre, go to a bar or an amusement park. Everything is in the new locket – served right there, while one stands still."

"No doubt! You are a master innovator – never off the mind of birds. Just see all the excitement here! However, a lot of birds also say that the lockets are getting tight around their necks and that is one of the reasons they are here. The locket, I hope, isn't a stealth strangulation device!" joked the reporter. And then realizing that what he said did not sound pleasing, he quickly asked his question: "Ah uhm! What do you have to say about that?"

"Ah! That is right. We have been observing that the necks of the birds have been consistently growing in size – becoming thicker every day. This is what makes the helpless lockets tight! But we are here to serve the birds at all times. We are providing them with new lockets to satisfy their ever-growing necks and needs," submitted Sboj.

"We all know how customer-focused you are. Your lockets are the highest rated by customers and surpass the demand of any other product sold on the trees. These long lines speak for themselves!" The reporter gestured to the long queues out there. The birds waved to the camera.

"Hail the locket!" Sboj shouted to the flock. The birds sent up an enthusiastically affirmative "Whoooop!" which carried to the next branch and the next until the celebratory cry became like a wave, washing over the trunk and down to the ground along the long endless zig-zag of birds.

Malika stood among the zigzag also, at a far corner, and she too hailed the locket with a shout. She waved it, high up her beak, as she jumped up and down. The locket started vibrating. She tapped it and it was Mustafa - uhm, that interrupted all the excitement!

"Where are you? We're supposed to go to Sheru's, right?" asked Mustafa.

"Oh yes! But the queue here is very long. I will take more time. There is so much excitement here! I have never seen the birds so happy. Why don't you go by yourself? Tell me what happens there."

"Uhmm, fine," said Mustafa feeling disappointed. "See you later." His wife had always been at his side - in his happiness and in his grief. He felt alone - very alone. He opened his wings and flew to Sheru's abode.

Sheru perched on his throne. Sopari sat to Sheru's left on a throne as high as his. Tima sat at the base of the two, peering intently into his locket. There was a throne to the right, this one made up of crystals. One couldn't see who sat there. A gigantic almond-shaped magic mirror stood in front of it. A bulbul sang and danced in the mirror, making suggestive moves with her long multi-colored tail feathers. She would blink her eyes and bat her long curled-up eyelashes, in a come-hither kind of way. Then she would turn around, sway this way and that way and wiggle her behind, fanning her long tail feathers.

All the other birds that used to be in Sheru's *darbaar*, were gone along with their perches.

Mustafa flew in, nodded to Sopari and then greeted Sheru: "Hello Sheru, how are you?"

 "Oh! Old fellow Mustafa. It has been such a long time. I hear you have become a rich man..." The voice did not come from Sheru! Mustafa looked here and there in confusion.

The voice called out again: "Look here!" It was Misho, right there at the top! She flapped her wings rapidly, stationing herself at a single position in the air without support. It was a feat that birds had tried for centuries, but never achieved – or may be one of them did. Misho had done it in a jiffy.

Sheru laughed heartily at Mustafa's confusion, hugged himself and tapped his head thrice. "It is me! I speak through Misho. My vocal cords were taken over by a disease some time back. But, Misho is a marvel – helps me speak! I am invincible. How are you? I hear your business is doing great. Do not need Sheru's help any more, don't visit Old Sheru anymore?" Sheru laughed again.

Mustafa felt overwhelmed with these strange goings-on. He regained his composure and spoke: "No, Sheru. Had gotten a little busy. But we talk about you all the time. Actually, business is not doing very well, so I thought I would come and talk to you." Mustafa took turns looking at Sheru and Misho while talking.

"Business not well? Isn't Mustafa candy the best across all the trees?" asked the mechanical voice sarcastically.

"Everyone across all the trees buy Goodweb candy now. All reflections are full of just Goodweb candy. My business is running out of money. My daughter doesn't have a job. I am confident I can put my business back on track. I want to borrow some money from you..." Mustafa lamented.

"Money, money for what?" clucked the voice.

Mustafa found it strange to hear such things from Misho. "Well, I will use some to improve the flavor of Mustafa candy to suit the taste buds of the new young birds. And put a lot more into getting some space on the crystals…"

"But, do you understand crystals and know how to control the reflections?"

"No, I do not," said Mustafa twitching his wings. Timidly he added, "I will hire birds that understand it and they will help me with it."

"It doesn't work that way!" Misho thundered. "You cannot compete with deadwood candy…"

"Goodweb candy," Tima corrected.

"Yes! Goodweb candy! They are such a delicious candy. I haven't tasted it ever, but all celebrities love it. And then they are the masters of the crystals. Everyone is hooked on to them!" said Misho.

"And they are such good people, splendid people, my good friends. How can I give support to people who would compete with them?" Sopari shook her head. Tima just chuckled, looking down at his locket.

Mustafa was dumbfounded. Misho came to his rescue, "Uhmm I have a different proposition for you, much more attractive. If you are interested, I am happy to share..."

"Sure, tell me..." asked Mustafa, twitching his wings.

"How about you sell Mustafa candy to Goodweb candy? I know them well, in fact, I had invested in them and can help you get a deal. Then you won't need to compete with them anymore. What do you think?"

"But, then what will I do?" asked Mustafa with surprise.

"Oh! They can give you a job at Goodweb candies. Maybe you can be a part of their taste department. Or you can become a dealer for their candies on your tree. Or maybe you can do both. We can talk to them about it..."

Mustafa was speechless. Haltingly, he replied: "I do not think I want to sell my business, my father..."

"There is not much left in your business, Mustafa," said Sopari. "Goodweb candy is the tastiest. I have never tasted it though ... It will be hard to convince Goodweb candies to buy your business in any case. They own all the reflections. Think of it like shutting your business, because you'll be lucky to get peanuts for it. At this age, you need to think about yourself. Secure yourself a job, get yourself some salary. We can add a little more for your wife. She needs the money. Take her on a vacation - she has been so wanting it," he paused, and then added, "All women want to relax at this age, you do not want to fight with her constantly."

Mustafa kept quiet. He felt helpless.

Tima held up his locket and grinned an evil grin. "Listen to Sopari, Mustafa. You dare disagree with us. No one disagrees with us. I can help you make a quick decision. Do you want to see the pictures I am seeing here, the lovely Moshi taking a bath... So sweet and chirpy! She is even more beautiful than her mother. Wow! The perfect belly! You want some fun. Let me get the reflections to carry it... Jaico's reflections can take them far and wide... they are faster than sunlight."

As Tima raised his wing to tap the locket, the gigantic mirror fell, shattered into pieces and Jaico emerged from behind. The dancing bird came undone in the pieces, disfigured, and then vanished completely. The sound of the collision rippled through the room, momentarily paralyzing the occupants with fright. Sheru and Sopari dove behind the throne, and Mustafa threw himself forward and covered his head with his wings.

Jaico smacked Tima down and struck him first with his claws and then his beak. As Tima screamed and wailed in terror, Jaico shouted into his face. "You pervert! You want all your pictures on the crystals, all the things you do with toys, your fetishes and all of it…where did you get Moshi's from… this is not why I share the trapped reflections with you… where did you find them?"

Sopari intervened and put her wing across Jaico's chest and gently backed him off the bleating and whimpering Tima. She counted ten deep breaths from Jaico's lungs and then began to speak.

"I am sorry for what he did, Jaico. Just leave him alone. He is a piece of shit. Don't waste your energy on him. I will teach him a lesson. Remember, I told you – people will do all kinds of things with reflections. You have been seeing that happen. You are not responsible for it. Don't take it personally. This won't happen again. You cool down…"

Mustafa, meanwhile, had crawled to a corner. He watched the proceedings in total bafflement. Tima's words about Moshi still echoed in his ears. He dreaded what the tap could have done. Or could do in future? Jaico was such a saver. He felt relieved and safe for the first time in Jaico's presence. He struggled to his feet, his knees still shaking. Through trembling voice, he managed some words: "Hey Jaico, nice to see you! How are you? How come you are here?"

Mustafa's homely words had a calming effect on Jaico. He had blood in his eyes. He said with a decent demeanor, "I am well. How are you? I am collaborating with Sheru. He is funding some of my businesses. And then, he knows how to run the birds. I need quite a few to deliver the stuff, reflections can't yet move... the physical goods, food, and what not." Further, he said while kicking Tima with his claw, "and helps me manage pervs like these..."

"Ah, ah! I see. Nice fellow you are. Good, good! Nice to see you here. You are the ONE still holding on to the commandment 'Do no evil'...."

Jaico interrupted, "It was **DON'T BE EVIL.**" A silence came down over the room, which seemed to crowd out the ricocheting commotion.

Jaico continued. "Probably Bakru said it wrong. I am never evil. People may see what I do as evil. Or others may do evil things with my stuff... but I am not evil." Jaico was telling himself.

Mustafa moved quickly to assure him. "Of course, yes, you are not evil. Good fellow," he paused and added, "I am worried about Moshi. She is very young. Crystals are wrecking her life – my heart trembles, as I relive Tima's words. Moshi hasn't been home for some days. Did you see her lately? This is not the first time she is gone without saying, but it has been longer than ever before. I hope she is safe."

"Moshi! No! I saw her last three days back..." A gloom set on Jaico's face. "She has not been at home?"

"Oops! I thought she must be with you. I must leave now." Mustafa flew off.

Malika sat on a side, covered by projections from her new locket. The projections formed an impenetrable hemisphere around her. Music was playing from all sides giving her a theatrical surround-sound experience. She moved her wings rapidly, pointing upwards, downwards, sideways, in a different direction every time, as if pressing buttons in the air. Her eyes were glued to the projections in full concentration. It was not clear if she was in total control or rather being controlled effortlessly. One could imagine strings attached to her wings being moved around by a puppeteer. In between, messages from her friends would pop up, to which she would reply with single taps. And then a side glance would catch a glimpse of a lovely dress, a beautiful scarf or a candy and she would do a one-tap buy. While performing all of these great feats, Malika still wanted to be an informed individual. The "23 words" updated her continuously, now on an hourly rather than a daily basis.

Mustafa came in exhausted, physically and mentally. He called out to Malika twice, but received no reply. He looked down at the ground and was lost in contemplation. Where to look for Moshi? What to do about his business? What was going on with his life?

And suddenly, he felt as if everything around him was moving. His whole world was shaking! He looked at Malika – she sat absolutely as before, engaged in her activities. Was it only him seeing it, or rather feeling it? Was he stressed? unwell? having palpitations?

He flew out to get some fresh air. And lo, so many birds were out on the tree, all looking anxious. The world was indeed shaking! Their tree had just shaken wildly. Nothing like this had ever happened before. Some of the more inquisitive birds were crowding down at the base of the tree and examining it closely. Mustafa flew down to join them.

Sludge was pooling at the base of the tree – dense and ugly. The soil had turned various colors – blue, gold, green and silver. Some of the roots of the trees were visible in the soil. They were thin, discolored, and were rotting at the ends.

One bird remarked, "Oh my God, the soil is changing colors, the tree is possessed by ghosts!" Many in the group trembled at the thought.

Iota, an elderly bird, was carefully examining the soil and roots with a magnifying glass. She was pushed back by another bird. Clut. Clut. Clut. She clicked a few pictures with her locket. She flipped through them, added some effects to sharpen the discoloration and rot, and tapped the locket to send the pictures. The hourly update went with them: "Tree possessed by ghosts, stained by their blood, trembles..." She continued to gaze at her locket, sometimes getting excited, then dismayed and then excited again...

Mustafa approached the bird with the magnifying glass. "Iota, what do you see with your magnifying glass. What happened here?"

"The soil has become contaminated and that is poisoning the very roots of our tree. The soil density is low, which weakens its hold on the tree."

"And why is that happening?"

Iota replied, "It is all the waters which we use in our homes, which finds its way down here. We use too many chemicals in our soaps, in our cooking, in our washing and even the food we eat. They all flow down and accumulate here. They do not disintegrate themselves, like the natural things we used earlier. The nature can do with the dirt of our bodies, but not the dirt of our mind and its creations..."

A sweet-sounding voice from the back interrupted Iota, "But, Iota aunty, why did that make the tree shake suddenly, just for a bit, and why today? The chemicals and the degradation must be happening since long, right?"

"Oh! Moshi, how are you?" asked Iota. Mustafa suddenly felt his world had returned to him. He hugged Moshi tightly.

Iota continued, "That is a smart question, like always, from your curious self. It seems something came and hit the tree, and the tree trembled due to its weaker roots... it could be a large animal who hit it, or a ghost like that little birdie was just saying." She winked. "Or maybe just a strong wind... But this is just the beginning, you will see this happen much more frequently and with much greater intensity."

The photographer bird still engrossed in her locket, looked up, as if her ears had captured an important update. She turned back to the locket and quickly tapped, "Tree was shook by the wind of the ghost of a large animal, says expert." And off went another reflection.

"So, what do we do now?" Mustafa looked perplexed. "Yet another uninvited problem!" he thought.

"Well, well, like we have the mesh of tubes providing us water, we will need to have another one to collect all the used water and dump it far away from all our trees, from where the chemicals cannot harm us."

"And where is such a place, aunty, which is far from all our trees, and where this huge mass of chemicals can be disposed, without hurting any of the animals and not just the birds, and which doesn't eventually affect us in some way..." asked Moshi. Iota looked at her blankly. Moshi had been maturing rather fast, thought Iota.

Mustafa decided to insert himself. "Well, all questions do not need to be answered right now... Iota, let me know what we must do about building the new mesh. I am happy to help. I guess I am going to have a lot of time. This looks like a useful activity - which the crystals cannot do!"

Mustafa turned to Moshi and patted her, "Moshi, let us go home. We need to talk."

As soon as they entered home, Malika came running toward them and exclaimed, "The reflection just showed up a trembling tree. It looked very much like our tree. Is it? I never felt it - my world has been so calm - when did it happen? And it says the tree is possessed by ghosts..."

"Yes, yes it was our tree. It is not the ghosts. Iota says it is some chemicals... well that's a long story..." Malika looked at Mustafa in disbelief. Was he contradicting the reflections? Preposterous!

"See who I have got with me..." and he took Moshi by her wing and pushed her forward.

"Oh! Moshi, where have you been? We were worrying about you!" Malika clasped Moshi in her wings.

"No, there is nothing to worry about. I am doing well and in fact feel fulfilled. I spent some time on the tree of poverty and the tree of exploitation. There is much to learn by observing the problems in the world of birds up close. Sometimes, I felt dejected. But mom, your Matma book has kept my spirits high. Also, we can do with some of your teaching skills there. Do you have time from your classes?" Moshi started rattling in excitement.

"No classes anymore. All the kids are learning from the videos of great teachers from the other trees, carried by the reflections. They do not need me anymore. And really, I do not need them! I love my own world of reflections... Why don't you also use the reflections for your teaching requests... There has never been a better time for education – all knowledge at one's fingertips - no need of intermediaries!"

These were strange words coming from her mother. "Mom, data doesn't show that overall student learning is improving. Neither school birds nor college birds are faring any better than they used to. Are you sure students learn better through the videos carried by reflections?"

"Students are better engaged through reflections. It is the right medium. Classrooms are boring." Malika answered definitively and signaled her lack of interest in further conversation on the subject. She turned to Mustafa, "And what happened at Sheru's?"

Mustafa became glum. "Well, well! Not only did I meet Sheru, but also Sopari, her Tima and good old fellow Jaico. And Misho was also there. Long story short, they want me to sell our candy business to Goodweb candies and take a job with them." He rolled his eyes. Then he whispered, "And that Tima said some things..." Mustafa stopped himself.

He continued, "My father started this business... but now it is all a loss. Ugh, what to do?" He sighed.

"Goodweb candies taste the best," said Malika matter-of-factly, "I am sure Sopari must have requested Goodweb candies to give you a job. Sopari is such a saint, I saw her on the reflections recently and she reminded me of Matma." Malika looked at the unkempt figure on the wall.

Moshi raised her voice in protest, but was cut short by Malika, "Do not get started again... You have been mixing up with the wrong people... the traitors. They are a bad influence on you. Sopari is an *avatar*, she will emancipate us. Why acquire sin by criticizing her." She turned to Mustafa, "You should take the job. Goodweb candies taste the best. I cannot repeat myself enough. And we need the money." Malika's locket vibrated again, and she tapped another one-tap buy.

Mustafa looked at Moshi. Moshi remained silent. Did not utter a word. He felt resigned and defeated. "OK... Let us go tomorrow to Sheru's for further discussions."

Malika was no longer listening. She was already gone in her hemisphere of reflections.

"Moshi, I need you to come with me. I need someone by my side. Will you?" asked Mustafa. Moshi nodded.

And then Malika screamed. "Oh! it was Sopari who held our tree and saved it from falling. The reflections show it all... She is our savior from all the evil forces - known and unknown!"

That night Mustafa sat in despair on the balcony of his house. A house he may have to sell off soon. He felt an intense desire to talk to someone, to talk about how the times have changed for him. Who could it be? Suddenly, he remembered Sherman. Sherman was a wise man, a friend of his father's and a patron of his family candy. He wasted no time, spread his wings, and flew down straight to Sherman's tree.

Like always, he entered Sherman's house-cum-shop without announcing himself. He had visited here as a kid and he never needed to ask or take permission.

Sherman was frozen in a corner undisturbed by the cacaphony of his entrance. Even Sherman? Lockets again, he sighed. As he turned back to the door to leave, a shine coming from one end blinded his eyes. It was Sherman's 5X10 toy table. His curiousity got the better of him. He flew towards the table to find, once again, lockets of many different colors nicely arranged in a grid. The cats, the birds, the squirrels, were all gone, driven away by the shine of the lockets. "Lockets yet again!" sweared Mustafa.

Finally, he caught Sherman's attention, who was peering in a small old book, with his grandfatherly specs.

"Oh Mustafa! How pleased to see you. It has been ages... I am sorry, I didnt see you come in. This is a very interesting book," he said pointing to an old red binded book. "It took all my attention. This is how books are. You forget everything around and the world. But no one is interested in books these days - no one buys them - so I have all of them to myself to read. How are you?" asked Sherman.

"Thank God it is a book! I thought it is the locket, the crystals, yet again. Can we chat for a bit. I really wish to talk to you."

"Anytime!"

Sherman quickly fixed some tea for both of them and sat in front of Mustafa, inviting him to speak.

"I am ruined, Sherman, ruined. Nothing in my life is working. My business is dead. My wife is no more interested in me, but only in her world of crystals. My daughter doesnt have a job and what can I say – her honor is compromised," Mustafa bursted into tears.

"Take it easy Mustafa." Sherman tried to comfort Mustafa, "Have some tea. And tell me everything from the beginning."

Mustafa sipped his tea, regained his composure and started, "No one is interested in Mustafa candy anymore. Everyone is going after Goodweb candy. All the reflections carry just them. I have no business. Sheru wants me to give up my business for peanuts and take some measly job. I have no money, no savings..."

"And why no savings," interruped Sherman, "You have been running this business for so many years..."

"That is the sad part. When the reflection first came about, I got partners from several trees. I ramped up investements in Mustafa candies, bought machines, drove up marketing and employed more birds to help me out. That took away all the savings. And before I could get a payback for them, Goodweb candies were everywhere. Malika used to save big time, but alas! she has now become the biggest buyer on the reflections. She has bought more in a month than ten years of our married life..." lamented Mustafa.

"What happened to Malika? She was a splendid teacher? A knowledgable one – I always loved to make a conversation with her," asked Sherman surprised.

"Only God knows what happened to her! She is always in her locket. I had thought that now will be 'our' time. Moshi has grown up. But it is she and her locket. The teaching classes have stopped. No little birds show up at our home anymore. I long for the chirps, that once irritated me. I haven't seen her book shelf in ages. I shouldnt be complaining – good to have fewer things to move in a smaller house. Everything gone for a locket – I see you have also taken a fancy to them." Mustafa said with a smirk, pointing towards Sherman's toy table.

"Oh yes! I also long for the chirps. Even, when the little birds show once in a blue moon, there are no chirps. Their innocence is gone. They know a little too much. Good for them!"

Sherman picked a locket from the table, "All they like is these multi-colored lockets. None of them wants toys these days. All the toys are in these lockets! I wonder how they will ever know how to use their wings to do anything. Or learn to play with other kids! Uhmm! Toys remind me of Moshi and the little bird she bought from this shop once upon a time – what did she call her? Moshu? What happened to her – she was a bright young girl." asked Sherman.

Mustafa replied, "Yes, she *is* very bright. She is my life. But can you believe it. That toy bird, she called her Misho, she took her job and is now an ally of Sheru! Why did that scientist ever make it. Why did you ever offer it in your shop. Why did Moshi ever chose it! It all seems like destiny today."

"It is not your destiny alone. This is the destiny of the birds. Few birds write the destiny for us all. The scientist who created Misho had become crazy popular. In huge demand. At one time, he was working with Jaico for some huge sums. But last I heard, he has gone nuts. Says, birds are using the toy birds in ways they shouldn't have. The toy birds have gone amok. They are using the birds now! In a crazy frenzy, he tried to use the reflections to erase the intelligence of all toy birds. Did not work. Knowledge once known is known. Poor fella!"

"Things do not get erased. Once there, they are, they remain." sighed Mustafa. "Can I tell you something? It weighs me down. Do you promise, it will remain with you?" Mustafa looked at Sherman who nodded reassuringly.

"You know Tima? Yes, Sopari's minion. He was looking at some rather uncharitable pictures of Moshi... He had got it from the reflections. Jaico stopped him, otherwise...  it would have been passed on to all the reflections. Oh! My daughter..."

Sherman clasped Mustafa with his wings and comforted him, "Don't worry for what did not happen. They never went on to the reflections, right?"

Mustafa said in despair, "Once it is there on the reflections, it is. It cannot be erased. It will pop up anytime and destroy my daughter. What must I do? A man with no earnings, no family and a daughter with no future..."

Sherman looked at Mustafa thoughtfully and then said, "Don't feel so low. Things will look up. Times change and we have to change with them. Little birds stopped coming here. They didnt want toys anymore. I pretty much decided to shut my shop. My assistant said he wants to sell multi-colored lockets – that is what the litte ones want. I let him do that. I have engrossed myself in my books. What a pleasure – after a long time, I have all the time in the world to read..."

Sherman picked up the red binded book, "And this one is a rather interesting one. It talks about animals in a farm who revolt against the ruler to become free and equal. Yet, they find the new world is no better. Of course, we are a way superior species than animals, but sounds much like our world after crystals. There is a character..."

Sherman read Mustafa's disinterest  and concluded, "Long story short. Times change. I have changed with time. Once things settle down, you may cherish all the time you have and do interesting things with it. It may be a blessing in disguise. And don't worry about Moshi. I am pretty sure she will do well... such a bright girl."

Mustafa nodded. His situation was very different from Sherman's – Sherman was at the end of his life, Mustafa wasn't. He couldnt just be reading books! Yet, he had a load off his mind by speaking to Sherman.

He got ready to leave. As he flew towards the door, his eyesight caught a little bowl by the cash counter. It had Goodweb candies in it.

The sun was out. The sky was bright with light. Birds filled the sky, as they do in the morning. But they weren't flying, chirping, or in a formation or teasing with each other. They were frozen in their places in the sky, with their eyes on their lockets. They were looking at reflections - rather their trapped reflections held their physical being in place. The lockets had succeeded in their mission. The static birds' silhouettes cast a dull look on the trees, which now all looked the same - no difference, no activity. Little newborn birds sat alone in their nests, some dozing, some crying and some looking at shiny lockets, waiting endlessly for an opportunity to play in the sky, to go up, fall down, and rise again.

Down under, in Sheru's den, there were rows and rows of mirrors. A lot of activity went on even at this hour in the morning. Mirrors were being rotated, tapped and spoken to. Here, little birds were flapping their wings, chirping in action. All unreal learning birds, like Misho. They were learning to control the reflections - learning through the patterns they observed on thousands of reflections and predicting how real birds would respond to their actions on the reflections. Every minute their control on the reflections became larger and they were becoming greater friends – panders – of the birds glued to reflections.

A buzzer on one of the birds went off. Jaico approached and inspected the mirror in front of it. He rotated it several times, up and down, coarsely and finely, and examined it intently. He plucked the bird and pressed various buttons on its belly. He then returned the bird to its place and observed the happenings on its mirror for several minutes. He flew back to Misho and said, "Good for now. I will work a little more on it. You must go and help Sheru."

Misho smiled to him, while she reflected to herself, "This is the control room of my Bird Farm. I will control all the birds from here. They don't even know they live in invisible cages in my bird farm. So much for them to think of themselves as a superior species, flying high and free!"

Misho flew outside to the **darbaar**. Sheru, Sopari, and Tima sat in their usual places. Mustafa, Malika and Moshi came in about the same time.

"Mishooo..." said Moshi emotionally.

"My name is Moshi," said Misho in Moshi's voice. Moshi was left stunned.

Malika bowed to Sopari devoutly and turned to Sheru, "Good morning, Sheru..." She wore her scarf with red and blue laces.

"Good morning, lovely lady," said Misho in Sheru's voice.

Malika looked up from Sheru towards Misho, confused.

Misho pointed to Sheru. "He talks through me."

Sheru glanced at Misho with a raised eyebrow – as if Misho had spoken out of chance.

The introductions settled, Mustafa began to speak with a sullen face. "I thought about it hard. I appreciate the gesture to help me. Sheru, I am willing to sell Mustafa Candies to Goodweb candies..."

"That is a great decision," Misho interrupted in a celebratory tone. "Congratulations for making such a wise decision. I knew it! You have a wise lady by your side. We will put all the power of reflections behind Mustafa candy... I mean the *new* Goodweb candy, once you guys are a part of the business. Only birds who understand reflections can run a business today. You will be in safe hands."

"But, you also don't understand reflections," interjected Moshi.

"Oh, but no one can do anything to me. I will continue to grow because *'r is more than g'*. I am CAPITAL. No one can fight capital in the bird sanctuary. I fund the controllers of reflections. Whenever the next revolution happens – I will be the one who funds its outcomes as well. I am invincible."

Mustafa wished to keep the conversation on track. He needed the job, the little money he could get. He didn't want to be upended by the imprudence of young Moshi. "Thank you," he didn't let his sarcasm be visible, "and what will the terms be?" he asked.

"I have already discussed with Goodweb candies. They want you both, you and Malika. They will pay a small amount for Mustafa candies – mostly taking care of any debt it has. You will be working in the taste department of Goodweb candy. The salaries in the taste department aren't the highest, but they will work out something reasonable for you. They would want to use your creativity and they love the study Malika did for your candy..."

"But, Goodweb candy is already the tastiest, why do they want us in the taste department?" asked Malika, looking up from her locket.

"Uhm! Because, Goodweb candy can be made even tastier. We want to make it such that little birds want one always in their mouth. Be never without them..."

"OK! More the birds, larger the experiments, better the candy becomes, more birds thus eat them and thus it goes on. But I keep very busy. I can only work for half hour a day," said Malika with a whiff of importance.

"That is fine. You have nice reflections... all the rapid wing movements... I get hooked to them... err..." said Sheru, tapping his head thrice. And then he added in an off-hand manner, "And you must handover the recipe of your candy to them. There is no deal without it."

Mustafa nodded blankly.

Tears of joy ran down Sopari's face. She took charge of the situation, "I am glad I am alive to see this day. The true power of crystals has finally manifested. So nice to see birds are getting jobs, in large crystal companies, such as Goodweb candies. And female birds are also getting a place in the job market. How wonderful! That is what I have been working towards all these days, to touch the last bird in the bird farm... argh... the bird world... with the power of reflections. My efforts arc finally bearing some result. The revolution which

Bakru talked about is coming to life in front of my eyes. This is an emotional moment for me, and I didn't let it go!"

Sopari raised her locket and a projection of Sheru, Sopari, Mustafa and Malika showed up, with joy on every face and tears in Sopari's eye. Misho was missing. She kept away from public view.

"As all of you made this historic decision of friendship and togetherness, I sent it to the reflections... what a story! Wonderful things happen when Sopari, Sheru and Jaico come together. Sopari giving the right inspiration for the welfare of birds, Sheru bringing the right opportunity and Jaico the power of crystals. Mustafa and Malika, you are so lucky to have such birds around you. What a happy ending... err... beginning." Surprisingly so, the reflection looked more joyous than the sullen mood of Mustafa and the disinterest of Malika.

All reflections on the day carried this picture with a ten-word update, "Revolution has happened. Birds have been saved. Long live Sopari!"

A smile appeared on Malika's face as she peeped in her locket. It soon turned into elation. It was her luckiest day... to be in the same frame as Sopari! It indeed was historic.

Jaico flew into the festivities. His face lit up on seeing Moshi. There was an awkwardness, but he finally spoke up, "How are you, Moshi? Where have you been all these days?"

Moshi responded pleasantly. "I am well, Jaico. I have begun living on the tree of poverty and spending time on the tree of exploitation. How are you?"

"I am fine. Too much work, too much pressure. All the funders, Sheru, Sopari, they want to grow the crystal empire very very big and powerful... Good to see your parents join Goodweb candies. I have been helping out the company for some time now." He continued, "Crystals will change the life of the birds. Always, working on it. What have you been up to?"

"I am trying to understand problems. I can do so, only by being close to the birds facing the problem. I am trying various experiments and studying how they help, what works and what doesn't. I am *learning*."

"Oh! that was what I had planned with my charity..." Jaico began, but was promptly interrupted.

"Jaico, your charity was about solutions and crystal solutions only. I am trying to understand problems. Without understanding problems, how can I think of good solutions? I am also learning about crystals and reflections and how they work. They would definitely be a part of the solution but aren't the full solution in themselves. For now, we are having some problems with lockets and reflections - a lot of our birds, both little and grown-ups, spend a lot of time on it just doing NOTHING," quipped Moshi.

"All this sounds great. I would love to help. To begin with, let me get all the crystals to reflect your work... it will create interest..."

"Hold on, Jaico! Not required at this point. There is much to be done. And I will need your help, especially to understand how we can run experiments with reflections to solve our problems. I will call on you myself, when I need you. And I will need you soon."

Jaico smiled and nodded affirmatively.

At this point, Bakru flew in. A patch was stuck on his crown and a wire came out of it. At the other end of the wire was a learning bird. The bird was half flesh and half metal. The flesh half didn't look like any bird seen to-date. Bakru spoke through the hybrid bird, "The birds are moving ahead, beyond the reflections and the crystals. We will now tap into the reflections in the minds of birds and alter them. We will grab the reflections in the soul of the birds and play with them. Birds will become most powerful! We will conquer all diseases. We will conquer DEATH. A new revolution is coming..."

Mustafa retorted back, "And what must you say about the crystal revolution?"

"I see, right here, the Ruler of Crystals, the Ruler of Minds, and the Ruler of Fortune, all come together. And with them the learning bird. Each is very mighty and together they are ALMIGHTY. But who is the mightiest of all? Each is suspicious and insecure of the other's power. They will fight to find out. They will hurt each other. Revolution will happen. It must happen."

Bakru hung his head in shame.

# EPILOGUE

The morning sun rays brightened the trees of poverty and exploitation. The rays reflected through the thousands of dew drops spread across the leaves, dropping from their edges and meandering and dancing down the trunk. The drops all looked like crystals. The trees were shining.

Moshi was surrounded by a few little birds. A mirror next to her played a video. It showed how to analyze data and make inferences. Young birds raised their hands if they did not understand a part. Moshi would pause the video, provide explanations and then let the video resume. She would make detailed notes after every other question. The video continued for fifteen odd minutes. Then, Moshi took out worksheets and distributed them to all the young birds.

"My little learners, here are questions for today's lessons. We will spend the next hour solving them. The first twenty minutes, each one of you will work individually on the worksheet. During the next twenty minutes, you will pair with the bird sitting next to you and help each other on the questions where you got stuck. The next ten minutes, the pairs will pair again to work on the remaining unsolved questions. And in the next five, the quadruples will pair and so on, till as a group you address all the questions."

The birds began to work on the sheets. Moshi went from bird to bird, looking at their sheets to see how they were addressing the questions. She really enjoyed seeing the different approaches the birds used. She also closely observed where they got stuck - this helped her design her lessons better. And here she found Kuz going in the wrong direction.

She pointed her beak to a line on his worksheet. "There Kuz, that is where you started going wrong. You cannot use that data in solving the question. The question says you cannot use personal information."

And then she came across little Druva, who had made very little progress - just two lines written.

"Druva, what happened? Seems like you are still just getting started."

"I don't understand these things. They are not for me," he replied looking down.

"Why do you think like that?" asked Moshi puzzled.

"All the birds here are very smart. I am not. None of the birds in my family are smart. We aren't intelligent birds."

"No Druva, birds that make an *effort* do great things. Birds are successful because of their hard work and effort, not their smartness."

Druva hung his face - responding to as-if empty motivational talk.

"Uhm! You know of a friend of mine - no one thought he was smart, maybe he didn't himself, either." Moshi paused. "But he put in a lot of effort. Do you know who I am talking about?"

"Who?" Druva looked up curiously.

"Jaico!"

"Jaico! He is God! He is your friend? What are you saying - people thought he wasn't smart?"

"Yes, indeed! I will ask him to come sometime and meet all of you. He will learn a lot from you, learners. Now, let us look at the first question here... Let us take it slowly. So, do you remember how we calculate the mean... No? how about average?"

Druva nodded and said, "sum all the numbers and divide by the total number of numbers..."

"There you go. So, you have to calculate the average..." and Moshi and Druva got into a conversation. And like this, Moshi moved around the class helping the birds and learning herself. Birds paired up, and paired again, till they all were one.

At the end of the class, Moshi took centerstage. "You all have done very well!" The young birds were beaming. "Do you know why?" asked Moshi.

"Because we are smart," said one of the birds

"No, because we put effort," Druva butted in, in his thin voice.

"Yes indeed, because all of you make effort and are hardworking. This is indeed the one lesson, you should remember, if you forget all the others you learned here."

She continued, "We will be soon completing the full course. We will then help you get jobs that suit you, as per your learning and interest. But, not to forget, you all need to become helper birds other than doing your job. There are numbers of birds across the trees who are where you were, when you started these classes. We need to help all of them learn. I am not needed. You need to replace me, incarnate me a hundred times and pay your debt."

With that, Moshi glided down, and down, to a very low branch. Three unusual birds lived here. The first, Tira had faced severe abuse on the reflections. But mental agony alone was not an adequate punishment for her great folly. She had tried to fight the reflections by airing a view different from the TRUTH that most reflections carried. Eventually she was identified, traced and beaten up. She lived only because she was mistaken for dead.

Suru was kidnapped from her nest on the tree of oil, to the horror of her parents. She serviced and pleasured a hundred, no exaggeration, birds over the next six months. She lost all meaning in life, till one day she was rescued.

And there was Hina, the beautiful one, whose best friend shared her pictures and videos in compromising positions, on the reflections. She was mocked and taunted every day by her friends, classmates, and yes, her family. Her only choice was to run away from everyone who knew and had ever loved her.

A creeper had climbed its way up the trunk of the tree. One offshoot had come to the branch with the three birds. It had beautiful flowers. Moshi tied the end of the offshoot to the branch to make a wide swing. Moshi, Tira, Suru and Hina all hopped on it and started swinging to and fro, from one horizon to the other. As fresh air swept through their wings, they felt delighted... away from all the happenings of the world, as if they were flying again! As they swayed the branch, droplets of dew sprinkled over them from the leaves above – they chuckled – dissolving the trauma of the past in the nature's caring droplets.

Though cheered, they soon grew impatient and hopped off. They had to get down to work. Tira's book was near completion – she was challenging that reflections were the truth, once again. She argued that reflections by their very nature multiplied falsehood, propaganda and sensationalism. Her arguments were inspired by Matma's ideas. Even seventy years after his death, his views remained relevant. Of course, it was a tall task to take the book to a critical mass of readers.

After all, publicity relied on reflections! It was on this aspect that Moshi helped Tira.

Suru worked to rehabilitate victims of exploitation, helping restore their honor in their own eyes and of the society. She had studied extensively how to counsel the birds and heal their wounds. She had made her organization into a lab, investigating scientifically what techniques worked and what didn't. She continuously iterated to develop new methods and tools to help birds integrate back into society. She had even found use for the learning bird!

Hina worked on a policy paper on the ethics of reflections. What were the all-powerful reflections permitted to carry and deliver, and what not? Who decided this! The community? The government? The firm? Or the individual? And what of the people who trapped millions of reflections? Who or what would keep a check on their power? Hina wasn't content just being in the oasis of her branch with its protective shades of lush green leaves, beautiful flowers and contemplate these questions. Rather, she wanted to vigorously try out her ideas, pilot them and work with the rulers of fortune, the rulers of the mind and rulers of the crystals, so that the solutions might someday see the light of the day.

Moshi worked with all the three birds. She was their pillar of strength. She learned from each of them, contributed her own ideas and leaned on them to think how they could best create big impact - help all the birds across the many many trees, not just one or two of them. After all, as much as the existence of suffering brings great discomfort to the social mind and great unease to the philosophical soul, it is also the progenitor of change and seed for excellence among birds. Moshi hoped that her friends' suffering would ultimately bring good.

Tira turned to Moshi and said, "I have been wanting to ask you something for a long time. You suffered due to the reflections and so did I. They spread lies, bring down productivity, take away jobs and break lives. Why do you then, my friend, use reflections in your classes and teach skills that power the reflections. Have you compromised with this big bad world?"

Moshi smiled, "Life is imperfect by design - it is a compromise. But no, no compromise with reflections. New technology comes and will continue to come. Birds need to and must continue to innovate. The problem is when birds think that such new technologies will lead to a revolution solving all of the birds' problems! Revolutions shift power from one set of power-groups to the new ones it creates. They do not democratize power, they do not democratize opportunity, they will not make all birds happy in a jiffy. All technologies have inherent in themselves the good and the bad. What matters is our collective intent. We will continue to have birds who want power, control, wealth, all of it. Technology doesn't change that. Technology could both be a helpful tool or one to amplify evil intent.

"Birds need to frame the right policies to tame technology to good use. This is what Hina is doing and you are doing. Birds need to understand both their problems and reflections deeply, to understand how reflections need to be used effectively in the context of the problems. Reflections are not the solution, but a part. I do not say this will solve everything. But this is the best we can do in our little imperfect bird world. That is what I am trying to do. I do not reject reflections, but I do not romanticize them either!"

Suru was waiting for her turn impatiently, "And I must tell one secret today. It is the reflections that saved me. I got hold of a locket that helped me send my location to the reflections. And I am now using the learning bird... new technology!"

Moshi looked at the angle the branch made on the tree trunk – it was time to soar high, to one of the undiscovered and unknown branches towards the top, where there was complete silence, just the sound, rather the voice of nature. She relaxed on this branch and flipped open a book to the page where she had left off. It was about inequality of wealth among birds: the richest birds got richer every year, yet quite a few birds were also lifted out of poverty. The birds seemed divided among the doomsayers and the optimists. What a paradox, she thought! As she ended her reading for the day, she wondered about the birds in the middle – neither the super-rich nor the very poor. What fate awaits them? That reminded her of dad. She opened the flap of her bag and took out her locket. This was the only time of day that she used it. All other times it would sit silently in her bag.

She rolled the sphere and tapped it. A projection of Mustafa came up.

"Hello dad, how are you?" asked Moshi.

"I am fine. But there is some bad news. Just returned from the funeral of Sheru. It was very sad to see him go away..."

"Oh! What happened?"

"The disease from his throat spread to his whole body, to his eye, his tongue, his wings, crippling all of them, till it took away his soul. Very very sad..."

"I am very sorry to hear. Hope he rests in peace. How is your project on the tubes coming along, the one with Iota aunty?"

"Ah! It is going very well. In the morning, I work on my candy machines. I'd like to create a museum with them. They do no work now - only good as a sight! That leaves the evenings to work with Iota. We have created quite a bit of the mesh, covering seven trees around our area collecting all the water that falls from the bird houses. Iota has put filters at the branch ends where the water drains. All the chemicals are separated and pushed into a deep pit. The bigger battle is to use less chemicals in our everyday chores. What they must be doing to our bodies, if this is what they are doing to the soil and plants! Oh, my my, much work to do for the birds!" Mustafa twitched his wings.

"Uhm! Seems like you have your hands full. Please do find some time to relax as well. Is mom around, can I chat with her?" asked Moshi.

"Oh! She is in her hemisphere. She recently became a sensation on the reflections. So many reflections just carry her and her updates. Sopari immediately got interested in her large presence on the reflections. They have been partnering. Did you hear, Sopari won the election again by a huge margin, more than anyone ever before. They say, she will rule for twenty years."

"I heard," Moshi sighed.

"And how have you been. Always working or getting some time to rest."

"I am very well, dad. Work is rest – it rests my mind. Otherwise my mind gets overwhelmed by imperfections..."

"My, my, you really have inherited some of your mother's flair! Talking in a language that I don't quite understand... or appreciate... oops."

"Hehe, no worries dad. I need to speak with another person now. You take care, bye!" said Moshi

"Take care, my little daughter."

And Moshi turned the sphere again and tapped it.

"Yes indeed. I bought one of the first learning birds you built for experimentation... Well, I had a rather funny experience with her. But that is another story... Hehe... These days, I teach little birds on the tree of poverty. However, I don't want the organization to be just dependent on me and my teaching hours, I want it to extend to thousands of trees. I am experimenting with peer learning... Yes, the results are good. I have been wondering if the learning bird can provide feedback to my learners based on what they do in their assignments and worksheets. That is where I spend most of my time and the videos do not help. If the learning bird is able to do that, then we can scale to thousands of trees... Yes, I am happy to host your visit here, try out things and work together... Yes indeed, Jaico is my friend. He will help. Even though he has very little time. The money is pocket change for him."

Moshami retired to her house after a long day of work. Every day was similar. Like this. Driven by dissatisfaction, yet very satisfying.

She had a smile on her face. Jaico was coming for dinner.

www.ingramcontent.com/pod-product-compliance
Lightning Source LLC
Chambersburg PA
CBHW051424150726

48000CB00005B/1949